37653009358253
Main Library
FIC CONNELLY
Crumbtown

MAR -- 2003

CENTRAL ARKANSAS LIBRARY SYSTEM
LITTLE ROCK PUBLIC LIBRARY
100 ROCK STREET
LITTLE ROCK, ARKANSAS

Also by Joe Connelly

Bringing Out the Dead

CRUMBTOWN

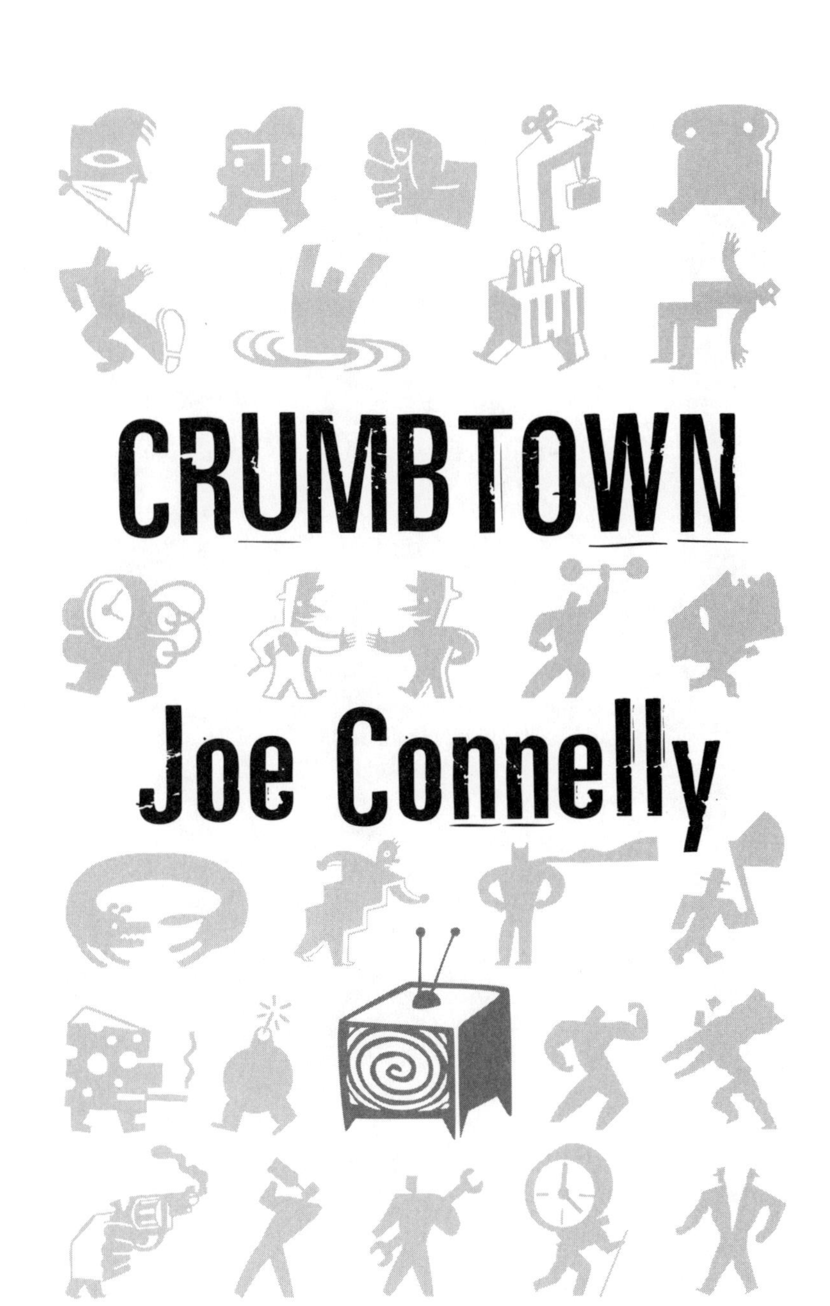

CRUMBTOWN

Joe Connelly

Alfred A. Knopf New York 2003

THIS IS A BORZOI BOOK
PUBLISHED BY ALFRED A. KNOPF

Copyright © 2003 by Joe Connelly

All rights reserved under International and Pan-American Copyright Conventions. Published in the United States by Alfred A. Knopf, a division of Random House, Inc., New York, and simultaneously in Canada by Random House of Canada Limited, Toronto. Distributed by Random House, Inc., New York.

www.aaknopf.com

Knopf, Borzoi Books, and the colophon are registered trademarks of Random House, Inc.

Library of Congress Cataloging-in-Publication Data
Connelly, Joe, [date]
Crumbtown / Joe Connelly. — 1st American ed.
p. cm.
ISBN 0-375-41364-2
1. Television programs—Fiction. 2. Bank robberies—Fiction.
3. Ex-convicts—Fiction. 4. Slums—Fiction. I. Title.
PS3553.O5115 C78 2003
813'.54—dc21 2002072930

Manufactured in the United States of America
First Edition

This is a work of fiction, about a fictional man named Don Reedy, who for several years robbed banks in and around the fictional city of Dodgeport, specifically in that imaginary section known as Crumbtown. It tells the stories that grew from those events, how those stories became legends, and those legends became television. Any nonfictional relationship between the characters in this book and other persons, living or dead, fictional or not, is completely coincidental.

CENTRAL ARKANSAS LIBRARY SYSTÊM
LITTLE ROCK PUBLIC LIBRARY
100 ROCK STREET
LITTLE ROCK, ARKANSAS 72201

CENTRAL ARKANSAS LIBRARY SYSTEM
LITTLE ROCK PUBLIC LIBRARY
100 ROCK STREET
LITTLE ROCK, ARKANSAS 72201

CRUMBTOWN

An Introduction

Don Reedy was a boy so briefly he often forgot it happened, no more time, it seemed, than it took a person to be run over in the street, but he remembered how proud he'd been, the mornings his mother sent him out for cigarettes, five years old and all the questions he owned: What do your hands sing? he sang to the men standing in front of the betting parlor; Why don't we fly? he flew to the old women elbowing in lines for buses. He cried when people tried to answer, because every answer took something away. His teachers in school were the worst thieves of all, who not only took what he asked but asked for his answers as well. By the time he was sixteen, he had only one question left—why should I go to school to be called stupid when I can be called stupid at home?

His mother called him much worse when he dropped out. "Is this some dummy I delivered?" she begged. "Now that I'm dying, I have to look at this?" He was dummy when he fed her, and when he walked her to the bathroom door. She had been calling him dummy for so long, what was she supposed to do, because she was sick she should be saying, Oh Don, oh my dear son?

Not in Crumbtown, where dummies like Don were a dime a dozen. They traced a long history, their missteps chronicled with pride, passed from one generation to another. Some of their brightest sons worked overtime at being dumb, on the streets after school, or in front of televisions sometimes late into the night, fractioning their vocabulary, multiplying their division—a period to end every question. All Don's friends except Lee, who sat in the front of class and said he was going to be a doctor, and who was eventually killed by a doctor, were quick to learn that no amount of facts would change the truth. Their luck had been bad before they knew what luck was. They'd grown up in a place where everyone was known to be stupid, and nothing they studied would ever get them born again in a smarter part of the city. Don's teachers had proven this with geographical algebra. His parents proved it by working themselves to death paying for a house made entirely of cancer-causing materials, a house that was sinking, like all the houses and people there, one and a half inches a year, into the river delta that had created Crumbtown ten centuries earlier, and was slowly taking it back.

At Don's mother's funeral, Uncle Joe the locksmith, who all day said nothing in his suit, burst out in big brown tears, and rubbed his arms on Don's, and offered him a job installing car alarms. In the following weeks, his uncle taught him the quiet beauty of keyless entry, the soft words every alarm system needs to hear. When Don got off the job at seven, he would go to work for himself. Two nights a week he'd take the bus to another part of town, a rose-lined driveway on Padlocked Hill, a spotlighted carriage path in Snob Gardens, where he would deftly part cars from their sleeping owners, without a note of protest from either. He took the biggest ones he could find, the silver and leather twenty-footers, drove them through the suburbs, the blackened landscapes beyond, then back to

Crumbtown, where he dumped them among the ghost piers lining the river.

One night Don picked up a glistening Eldiablo, only three thousand miles on it. He should have loved driving that car, but the forty-seven-position seats saddened him, the Aerosonic climate control left him lukewarm. Don could imagine the owner's face in the morning, finding the driveway empty, but what about later, waiting for the car to be found, or for a new one to be delivered. How would the man feel? He'd be waiting, looking ahead. Having your car stolen was bad luck, but it could happen to anyone, a throw-your-hands-in-the-air accident of fate. Don wanted the man to feel more chosen, the way Don felt every morning when he looked out his uncle's window.

He drove the Eldiablo to the shadowed end of Felony Street and he got out and stood at the edge and glared at the circling river, the bags of trash rising in the wake like rotting seals. Garbage. The smell was everywhere after a rain, in his hair, his hands. He fished out one of the bags and threw it in the back of the car and drove over to his cousin's garage on Marginal. Carefully he disassembled the dashboard and placed one empty sardine can behind the radio, then he opened the back of the rear seat and poured in a cup of old milk. He put the parts back together and drove the car up through the blossom-strewn streets of Padlocked Hill, cutting the engine and lights just before turning in the drive.

He found realarming the cars more difficult than disalarming, and returning them made the work three times as dangerous. Don didn't care. He felt so good that at first he thought he might be sick, some new kind of flu. Then it hit him. This was happy. A bit of Crumbtown in every part of the city. He had a breakthrough day when he installed loose marbles behind a glove compartment. He consulted other cousins, learned how to add miles to the odometer, how to interfere with radio reception by running the antennae wire through the engine block. Working five hours or more on every car, sometimes racing to get it back before dawn, leaving there to go to his uncle's locksmith job. While road-testing a burgundy Fort Worth to get the rattle in the vents just right, he fell asleep at the wheel. Next morning he awoke handcuffed to a stretcher. The nurse, who looked like Walter Cronkite, smiled while explaining how Don had crashed into the back of a police car, whose only occupant was taking his nightly nap. Don was lucky, she said, the cop was lying down when the Fort Worth struck. He'd have been charged with murder if the cop had been sitting up.

One year. Uncle Joe welcomed him home with a party of warm beer and some spilled mustard. You beautiful sweet idiot, he said. You dumb bird. They wanted to hear the stories Don didn't know, stories they'd constructed in his absence: how he managed to get the hamster into the mayor's air conditioner; the fish heads he'd left in the bishop's miter. He'd become a Crumbtown celebrity, nearly as popular as Tom Ramsey, who was doing a life term for shooting his mailman, and they cursed Don and laughed at everything he said. After all the chairs were broken, Maury Threetoes punched him in the arm and offered him a job stealing cars.

Within six months the little room at the top floor of his uncle's house had become a maze of new shoes and suits, so many colors he had to write them down to remember. Before he left for a job, he'd pick a suit that matched the color of the car he was about to steal, and before dropping it off in one of Maury's chop shops on Drywell, he'd take the car out to the clubs on St. Chevre. There he'd park and sit on the front fender, his shoes on the bumper, his pants raised just enough for the ladies to see, how his socks matched the upholstery. He kept a suede-covered book in the front pocket of his double-knit jacket, the names and numbers of fourteen business managers' daughters. Don told them he worked in a car dealership for a top secret government agency. This is happy, he thought, this couldn't be happier, until the night he met Tina Semple, who looked so much like her father, Judge Semple, the man who'd handed Don his first prison sentence, like it was a thing the judge cherished, something he wanted only Don to have.

Judge Semple's daughter, his dearest Tina, about to be number fifteen in Don's book, bent over the eight-track holder and giggled while she unzipped Don's canary-colored Robert Hall's. As he turned the car onto Washington, she lifted out Don's johnson, her fingers dripping down his leg, over the gas pedal. Don jumped the sidewalk and rammed the front doors of the precinct.

Two years. In his absence, Crumbtown sank another three inches, causing two more roads to become dead ends. Cancer rates, already the highest in the state, had risen ten percent, surpassing that of mice forced to live in similar surroundings. Duggin's plastics factory closed, and was demolished and replaced by a garbage storage facility. The last working port had been shut down and dismantled and sold to Tripoli. Ten Chinese restaurant workers were rumored to be living in the old Sanguina house, behind the Pig in Jelly.

Don rented a studio apartment over the welfare offices on Van Blunt. In the mornings he sat by the window and read the paper, the sports pages, comics, and eviction lists, the want ads for envelope salesmen and wig makers. The rest of the day he sat by the window and watched the men standing with their backs stuck to the liquor store window across the street, the old women waiting in groups of twenty or more at the bus stop on the corner. Uncle Joe the locksmith had moved up to Devon and taken most of his cousins with him, and Don spent the nights drinking beer with the few friends who weren't in prison, the half twins, Tim and Tom, Happy the Butcher, Iron Heinz, and Father Sunshine. He tried not to think about stealing, and thought about it all the time.

A month after his release Don was given a job driving deliveries for one of Maury Threetoes' four trucking companies. Every day before dawn Don would leave a warehouse on Lemon Street for the shopping districts on the northern side of the city. Three or four times a year, it had been agreed, he would stop at a certain diner and leave behind the keys. Later, on the phone with the police, he'd say he'd seen a Russian man driving away, or two Cubans, or three Chinese men dressed like restaurant workers. It wasn't stealing, Don told himself. He calculated that in twenty-five years he'd have been robbed as much as he'd robbed.

When his truck had been stolen for the second time, Don sat at the table by the window and ordered coffee, waiting for the police to arrive. He hadn't noticed the waitress setting down the cup, but when she returned for a refill, her hips blacked out all light from the window. Don looked up as her eyes turned blue, her lips and teeth white and red. He watched her walk away, then he raised his hands to where his heart had been, realizing he'd just been robbed again. The truck was gone, and now this waitress had taken everything in his chest. He tried to stand and speak, to tell her to bring them back. When the police came, he forgot the story he'd rehearsed. Instead of Chinese restaurant workers, he described the thieves as one young female, about twenty-two, wearing a white shirt and a white apron tied over tight black pants that showed the bursting seams of her underwear. Her face was a ticking time bomb, Don said, her brown hair waiting to explode out of her cap the moment she took off her shirt to take a bath. He warned the police not to look directly at her. The officer taking the report followed Don's eyes to the young woman behind the counter. He shook his head and, in his lined pad, wrote: *three Chinese males, mid-twenties, medium height, dressed as waiters, last seen heading north on Delinquency.*

Don returned to the diner the day after, with just enough strength to point to the coffeepot and groan as she poured from it. The next time he saw her, things didn't go as well, a shattered cup, a scorched foot, a clogged toilet, but on the third day Don finally asked for something to eat. "I'll have the leggs," he gasped, "over easy."

"I like your nose," she said, and wrote her phone number on the check.

Don never had trouble talking to women. He lied to them; he made up stories. His years in prison only made the lies easier. In fact, since his first sentence, the only times that Don could remember feeling comfortable was when he was lying to women. Along with everything else, she had taken that as well. How her eyes kept looking behind his, as if she knew the words before he could make them up. There was nothing left for Don to do. If he was going to say anything, it would have to be the truth, and the thought of that scared him more than any crime he'd committed. If she didn't run away, he'd consider himself engaged.

He picked her up the next day, in Happy the Butcher's rusting Beverly, and said little on the drive to the river. The way she looked at the car, at him, like he was made out of tin. He should have lifted that Manarey he'd seen three nights straight under the expressway, and put on one of those red suits that were just sitting in a truck in back of Maury's lot, waiting for the Brothers of Judgment to pay up.

For five miles she didn't say anything, through the long ramp up to the bridge and all the way across until they reached the other side, and then she didn't stop, how she'd noticed him the moment he first walked into the diner—he looked so sweaty and dangerous, she said, like he'd just stolen a car or robbed a bank. They took in a movie over in Haute Landing, and afterward she talked about the people they'd just seen shot on the screen. Together they walked past the car and into the park and sat on one of the benches facing the shore. Don was ready. He breathed in deep and clasped his hands, and began to tell her about his father, who was run over by a hook and ladder. His mother who never got better. His problems finishing secondary school, and the subsequent habit of driving new cars that belonged to graduates. When he reached the part about his first term in prison, Don hesitated a minute, and with the dismal constellation of Crumbtown flickering in the distance, he explained how the FBI had recruited him to help break up a sophisticated dollhouse of an auto-parts-trading pyramid scheme. For six months he was the youngest federal agent in the country. He worked as a cowboy to bust a ring of modern art rustlers, and was currently investigating a sneaker shipper selling smack to schoolteachers.

He finished the tale with his back to his date; his arms open to the collapsing tide. He lifted his head and felt a warm breeze near his neck, her fingers touching his. "Why is it," she said, "that all the guys I like are either cops or just out of prison?"

Don had known about jealousy; jealousy had left him sick, stupid, and imprisoned on more than one occasion, but it was different with a woman involved, more like a jagged lid you kept slicing yourself upon. He stopped going to the diner; the way she smiled at other men; the way she'd smiled at him. She couldn't see him on Tuesdays, Thursdays, and Saturdays. She couldn't say why. He'd get too upset, she said. He'd take it all wrong. For two months he carried the diamond he'd bought from his cousin's dentist. Don was determined to give it to her on one of the nights she couldn't see him. Mondays they fought with knives, Wednesdays with forks. Fridays she cooked him moussaka while he fingered the ring in his pocket.

When it came time for Don to be robbed again, he asked Maury Threetoes if he could have his truck stolen anyplace besides the diner. Maury said the diner was a charm. A businessman had to know a charm when he had one, and not be afraid to stick with it. Don drove his truck to the diner and sat three tables away from the guy who was supposed to steal it. He watched her bend over the guy's shoulder as she poured another cup. She hadn't seen Don come in. The guy kept saying things that made her laugh, and bring more coffee, though Don could see the guy wasn't drinking. Fifteen minutes he wasn't drinking. Don would steal the truck himself if he had to. He walked out to the parking lot and hit the horn three times. As long as the thief doesn't touch her, Don thought, he'd talk to him later, maybe on a Saturday, maybe he'd find them together. So that's why she couldn't see him. A woman who'd rather date a thief than a federal agent.

She saw Don come back in, and quickly she stepped away from the table, pulling her friend from his seat—the guy's hand still buried in her apron. Don walked into the kitchen and asked the cook if he could borrow a knife. He met her at the door, and placed the knife against her arm, and walked her behind the counter, and told her to give him all the money in the register.

"Don't be stupid, Don." She was looking over toward the guy whose hands she'd been warming. "He's a cop," she whispered. "What?" said Don. She mouthed the words again, but now the voice that went with it was a man's, and coming from behind Don's back. "He's a cop," said the voice, now accompanied by a gun near Don's head, a silver badge flashing before his nose, the same nose she once liked so much, that reminded her of a dead prince she'd known in high school. "She's trying to tell you I'm a cop, asshole." The gun was now inside Don's ear, the borrowed knife gone; his hands pulled behind his back. The cop pushed Don out the door and into the lot and up against the back of his truck, the gun still wedged in his skull.

"Well this is a pickle isn't it," the cop said. "How am I supposed to know that's your girlfriend. I'm having a cup of coffee and now we got fourteen people with window seats, the rest probably lined up at the phone to dial nine-one-one, and me just trying to make a few bucks on the side, off duty, and what am I supposed to do now, put you on a bus, can't take the truck, that fat Maury's gonna flip when he hears this, a romantic he sends me, turns a bullshit insurance scam into an armed robbery and me left holding the badge. I'll tell you what you do; make like you're grabbing for my gun and I'll shoot you and we can just forget this whole thing ever happened."

Don never heard him; with one ear pressed against the truck and the other pressing against the gun, he was thinking how well he'd planned these robberies, what Maury called staying three steps ahead of the crash. Don always parked the truck in such a way he couldn't describe the robbers' faces, only their ethnic background. He had staked out the diner for three days, and found that the local patrol always ate lunch there at exactly one-fifteen. Don liked to have the truck stolen at one, so that when the cops got the call they'd already be on their way. This put them in a good mood. They could take the report while ordering their food, and sit on the call for two hours while they ate.

Don tried to lift his head against the gun. Two hours, he thought, gave the cops plenty of time to chat with the waitress, take turns on the over-the-shoulder refills—he'd have something to say to them when they came, if they came—in a real emergency, you could never be sure. Don raised his arm to check his watch, heard a click in his ear, then a crash that turned light into black, as if someone had just broken the sun.

He awoke handcuffed to a stretcher. The nurse, who looked exactly like the *Today* show host Jane Pauley, explained how the cops on patrol that day had pulled into the diner around one-fifteen, thinking only of sharing a chicken, and found a man holding up another with a gun. The driver immediately reached for his own gun and crashed into a truck. In the ensuing disaster, an off-duty police officer broke his leg, a patrol car was destroyed, and Don, who suffered a fractured jaw along with assorted internal injuries, was charged with armed robbery and assault of a police car.

Maury Threetoes sent his nephews to represent the case, and to make sure Don wasn't talking about keys left in trucks for off-duty police officers to steal. Don had nothing to say. Besides, his teeth were wired together. When the clamps finally came off, Don still found the words wouldn't come, and for most of his sentence he spoke only in letters, *o* and *y*, sometimes *e*, sometimes in rapid succession. There's bad luck in the world, and then there's crumbluck, that's all he was trying to say.

Five years. The first words he spoke were to a young clerk in a liquor store in Tranquillity, words harder to say than he'd planned, "Gimme wheats in da dror and nobully will hurt." He said it two more times and still the clerk didn't move, Don reaching over the counter himself, a fistful of bills from the register, enough for breakfast, and one of Heinz's homemade .38s. He picked up a brand-new Bollinger outside Swab City, doing one hundred and five on the Old Iron Road. Never again would Don let himself be robbed, never fall in love, never return to prison. This time, they'd have to kill him.

Six months later he was standing in the lobby of the Dodgeport Savings and Loan, with Happy Jones, the twins Tim and Tom, all wearing the black masks that Mrs. Lasagna had sewn. On their way out, Don stopped at the line of customers, the worn-out men and women waiting patiently for him to finish. He stared at them for what seemed a long time, their bags of loose cans and bounced checks, a thousand years of fine print.

Don reached into his case and pulled out a bundle and threw it in the air, high as he could, the bills pulled up by the ceiling fans, swirling through the vaulted tops, the painted clouds, before slowly falling, arms and legs scrambling, fighting to the floor. He threw another thousand on the front steps, men and women chasing him to the street, the waiting car, bills tossed from the window as Tom drove away, his brother Tim grabbing at the case, the two of them screaming at Don to stop. Faster and faster. This is happy, Don thought, I've never been happier.

ACT I

Fifteen years later

One

SCENE I

Joe Far unlocked the door to the bar and held it open with a chair, to let in what was left of the morning and air out the last of the night. He filled the mop bucket in the sink, set the chairs on the tables, the stools on the bar, and rolled the bucket mop and broom into the men's room in the back. Through the dim light of the gated window he swept the used cigarettes from around the sink, the derelict pipes in the corner. The door to the bathroom stall was locked, the handle of a cane hooked over the top. Joe bent down and found the cane's owner sitting on the pot. "Wake up, Tim," Joe said, jabbing his broom into the man's legs. "Up. Get up." When the man didn't move, he took out the mop and rubbed it over the splintered tiles around Tim's feet, then he rolled the bucket out and closed the door.

"Joe, hey Joe." A bald man wearing a neck brace had come into the bar, and was sitting in the shadowed rear end, his stool tilted back into the surrendering paneling. "Get me a beer," the man said.

"No, Tom. We closed." Joe walked to the front door and shut it, slamming the lock.

"Come on, Joe," Tom said. "I need a beer, and one for Tim. He ought to be getting up soon."

Joe Far threw a glass that shattered a foot above Tom's head, a framed photo of a police lineup. "Now I clean," Joe said.

Tom adjusted his brace and walked behind the bar and pulled two bottles from the cooler. "Tim," he yelled, setting a stool on the floor next to his. "Beer," he said.

The bathroom door opened and the cane came out followed by Tim, who knocked down two chairs as he made his way to the bar. "What happened?" he said.

"You fell in there last night. We couldn't wake you up." Tom raised his beer and leaned his stool against the wall. With the brace around his neck, Tom could only drink at sharp angles to the floor. "We thought you were dead."

"Oh no," Tim groaned, "I can't keep living like this." He reached for the bottle in front of him, pressing it to his ribs. "What about my kids, Tom, who's gonna take care of my kids?"

"Who's been taking care of them?"

Tim sighed. He drank for a long time. "I have no regrets," lowering his bottle and lifting it again. "Just tell me one thing, brother, who was better than us?" He stood and banged his cane against the bar. "That's what I want to know. Who was better than us?" He walked to the back corner and hit the switch that lit a spotlight in the ceiling, shining a section of wall hung with newspapers, Tim reading from the top headline, "Robbing Hoods. Bank robbery turns into riot as masked gang tosses $$$ to crowd." The grainy photo beneath, of four men in black ski masks. "Tim and Tom Dwight, Don Reedy, Happy Jones. We were heroes, Tom. They can't ever take that away."

"We were kings," Tom said.

"You're right there, brother." Tim finished the beer and sat down, out of breath. He rested the bottle on its side, "Joe, help us."

Joe Far stood facing the window, broom in hand, and stared at the women clutching their bags at the bus stop, a man punching a pay phone on the corner.

Tim walked around Tom to the cooler behind the bar. The two men were half twins, same birthday, same father, different mothers. They had turned forty together three months earlier, and were still recovering. "Joe, comrade," Tim said, "my Chinese buddy pal. I need a big favor."

"No," said Joe Far, throwing a glass that crashed where Tim had been sitting.

"I need you to call Loretta and tell her I'm dead," Tim said. "It's better if she knows."

Joe swept furiously at the damp floor. "You owe me twelve bucks."

"It's in the will," Tim said. "Loretta will have it for you. My wife gets everything."

"What about me?" asked Tom.

Tim handed him a beer and placed another on the table near the cloud of broken glass that Joe Far was sweeping. "Please, Joe," Tim said, "call Loretta. Tell her I died."

Joe grabbed the remotes and pointed them at the television chained to the ceiling. On the screen, a rabbit was kicking a duck. Joe dropped the broom and lifted a cigarette from his Chinese army-issue raincoat, which in the five years he'd been sweeping there no one had seen him not wearing. He blew a series of smoke rings at the tarred tin ceiling.

2

Rob Landetta could get his hand on the front doorknob of his apartment. He could turn it. He just couldn't pull. Soon his boss would be calling, asking how come he wasn't in the office yet to pick up the contracts. Why wasn't he on the road already to Crumbtown, to sign up the woman too fat to get out of bed? Rob could understand how his problems with the door were simply the physical manifestations of his inability to write, yet this understanding did not bring him any closer to the computer on his desk; it only reminded him how many used and expired words awaited there. Twice in the past month, desperate for a solution, he'd left the oven on with the burners off, both times forgetting to close the window. The night before he'd been up until two talking to the angry lady on the suicide help line, asking her advice on the best way to die.

Rob was twenty-three when he wrote his first television pilot, *The Monkey House,* about homeless teens living in the Bronx Zoo. His "grit opera," which he directed himself, lasted two seasons, and was quickly followed by: *Black Tide,* clam diggers vs. oil refinery, half a season; *Veracruz,* hard-bowling vigilantes in a busted mine town, two episodes; and the short-lived *Death Valley Days,* snowbelt refugees on a desert oasis, canceled in preproduction. His last project, *Exley,* about a burned-out building inspector, had been cooling on the studio shelves for six months. He'd directed two deodorant commercials in the last two years, and was due to turn thirty in less than four months. Rob could see the other side of the hill now, the long downward climb.

To pay his rent, he'd taken a job with his former college friend Brian Halo, the third-biggest mass media superagent in New York, and worked as Mr. Halo's Fringe Client Outreach Assistant, the Freak Department. Rob paid visits to those who couldn't make it to the office, like the woman too fat to get out of bed, and other clients too deranged or delinquent to converse with on the phone. Rob made sure they signed the bottom line: Brian Halo Inc. gets one-third of all earnings, ninety percent of which goes directly into supporting the company director's lifestyle, documented for anyone to see on channel 63: *The Brian Halo Show,* every Friday at six-fifteen.

Rob tried the knob again, and fell to one knee in the attempt. There was a time when he used to start his days at six, sprinting five blocks to the gym, his next hour on the treadmill, wondering which girl to call, Ula, Tammy, or Kym.

He walked to the bedroom and pulled three sheets out of the closet and tied them together while listening to the TV, a song about powdering men's feet. He brought the sheets to the bed and tied one end to the frame and tugged at the knots, testing them, and threw the other end through the open window, his emergency exit. Before climbing out, he glanced back at the television he'd forgotten to shut down—Today on *Cheryl:* Women who kill their men.

"What's the point of writing," he shouted to the screen, "when everyone is writing themselves?" He walked down the wall, ten feet to the ground, threw the sheets back up to the window, and headed for the office.

3

Loretta dropped her arm off the pillow and groped for the phone. "Harbor Homes," she said, as if she was in the office already, instead of in bed. "Who is it? Joe Far? From the bar? Tim's dead? What happened? Listen to me, Joe. You tell him he has to sign those papers. I'm getting this divorce."

She heard the sounds of glass breaking downstairs, doors slamming, her daughters leaving for school. She put down the phone and picked it up again and called the police. "I need to speak with Detective Hammamann," she said, "yes it's an emergency. Hi Harry, it's Loretta, anybody kick last night? Oh Jesus," she said, grabbing a pen, writing down the name. "He lived alone, how big? A studio, huh, any light? I got an appointment at noon, you think they'll have him out by then?"

With the phone under her ear, she pulled a pantsuit out of the closet, held it up in front of the mirror, dropped it on the bed. She clicked on the television, a woman in a bathing suit was preparing to leap from a bridge. "No, Harry, I can't see you now," Loretta said, "I'm still a married woman, remember. I've got the girls to consider." She put a free ear against the bedroom door, listening for her daughters, to be sure they were gone. "Not until you take care of this thing, like you promised me you would." She bent over and reached under the bed, two shoes and some underwear. "No, Harry, there's no talking to Tim. His mind is gone. You said it yourself. That there was only one thing to do . . ." She waited through his excuses, the phone between her teeth, trying to be patient. "Just tell me that my husband is out of our lives, that it's just us, baby, me and you . . . now I got to go . . . no, Harry . . ."

4

Rita remained in bed the few minutes it took the framed border of the sun to descend the wall and cross the pillow to find her. When it left, she made the coffee, holding the cup to her stomach as she walked to the window's edge. She couldn't see the man sitting in the doorway across the street, three floors below, but she knew he was there, waiting to see her face, and if she took just one more step toward the window he'd be on his feet, crossing the street without looking, calling for his Rediska, come five thousand miles to beg her forgiveness, to bring her home.

Her name was Rita now, Rita Bell. She'd moved to a forgotten section of a lost city; she thought she'd disappeared. Six months later he was crying at her door, sleeping in the shelter of the alleys across the street, living out of an Aeroflot bag, brushing his teeth in the Mrs. Donut. The man who'd once been her shining husband, her proud, scowling Misha. He swore to kill himself if she refused to come back, or kill her and then himself, or both of them at the same time; he couldn't make up his mind.

She dressed beside the window, in order to see the far corner where the bus would eventually come and make its turn onto her street. An appointment with the real estate agent at noon, then to work in the bar. When the bus passed her door, she'd be out and running alongside, the bus blocking her husband's view, two blocks to the next stop. If he found out where she worked, he'd not only kill her but probably get her fired as well. "That is very funny," she said to the window, the bus starting its turn.

5

Rob crossed the makeshift bridge where Washington Ave became Lemmings, the recently restored cobblestones of Old Dodgeport narrowing into the double-parked potholes of Crumbtown. Four clients of Brian Halo lived there: Scarman, the dog swallower, the human fidget, and the still-to-be-signed woman too fat to get out of bed. Over the past six months, Rob had crossed that bridge half a dozen times, and yet no matter how well he steeled himself for the trip, memorizing the maps and bringing plenty of bottled water, he could never shake the need to flee that always struck the moment he entered. Fleeing was the only way to describe driving there, everyone leaving one accident for another, or leaving their cars wherever traffic stopped them, then running madly into alleys and empty storefronts. Every car was a ten-year-old sedan, many of them old taxis repainted and fitted with diamond-plated fenders, welded steel beams for bumpers. The men behind the wheel were made of corrugated tin, the backseats full of broken furniture and old women.

He passed through the corridor of Chinese fish stores and basement shops of secondhand gifts, and made his fifth right onto Low. The next block was cordoned off with a line of orange cones, a young man in headphones yelling at him to make the left. Rob ducked into his seat as he drove past the line of trailers and trucks marked wardrobe and props. He recognized Walter Yoshi, the director, walking toward an island of camera equipment on the corner. Walter had been his third AD on *The Monkey House;* now he was directing his own show, *Ten Thirteen,* which had started shooting in Crumbtown the year before. That was another reason Rob hated coming here—you couldn't drive five blocks without hitting some television drama moving up from New York. The production costs were much lower, and the network bosses said that the streets of Crumbtown looked more like New York than New York.

Back when Rob had an agent who answered his calls, he'd been led to believe he had a good shot at writing for *Ten Thirteen.* He knew Walter, and had worked with some of the cast and crew, but the producers went with the same old master's degrees from USC, who'd probably never been east of West Hollywood, and how did they expect anyone to believe Dyan Swaine as a police captain, that bulletproof chest she wore even to bed. The show was in the top five every year. Rob never missed an episode.

The light went red and Rob stopped and slid himself lower under the wheel, hoping Walter didn't see him. When it was green again, Rob raised his head and saw his former assistant standing in the windshield, "Hey, Wonderboy, what brings you to paradise?"

Rob looked up at the light. "Big things, Walter. The biggest."

"I saw that dwarf commercial. Great stuff. Hey, we're kidnapping Dyan Swaine today. You want to help me tie her up?"

"Thanks, Walter. Can I get through here?"

"Make a right, and then a left and then another left. You look stressed, Rob. I mean it's coming out in your skin."

Rob drove past the actors' trailers and the rows of cars with NYPD painted in blue and white on their side. Spending three million dollars an episode in a neighborhood where most of the residents were eating dog food. The injustice of it. Five hundred channels and no one would give him a job.

By the time he got around the set, Rob was lost. He couldn't find the fat woman's hotel, and the rental car he'd taken out of Halo's lot began to cry every time he stepped on the gas. Half the streets were unnamed, most of them dead ends; the houses numbered randomly. Three times he drove around the block he thought held the hotel, then all the blocks around that. After an hour of this circling, he figured out that the buildings were numbered not in sequence but according to color. He picked up the phone on the seat next to him and called Thelma at the office, who told him again the directions he'd already written down. "How many white buildings over from Dyre," he shouted, "white ones; that's what I need to know. I'm lost, Thelma." Still shouting as he ran the stop sign that someone had painted black. He swerved left around the crossing oil truck, cut right to miss by inches the back of the bus, and drove directly into the young woman running behind it.

Her head cracked against the windshield and the rest of her body came along to push the glass down and in, lines of cracked glass fleeing in all directions, her face looking at him through one hundred pieces. "Jesus," Rob said to Thelma, and kicked the brakes and watched the woman fly up and away, to reappear on the street thirty feet ahead, lying quietly, as if exhausted by a long fall.

He opened the door and approached her, the stocking torn around the knee, hands scraped pink and blue. Gently, he pulled the hair back from her face. The hundred pieces he'd seen through the windshield were put back in place. If he hadn't just struck her with his car, he'd almost believe she was sleeping, a beautiful woman sleeping in the street, an angel dropped out of heaven. Rob sat down next to the woman and watched the cars passing without pausing. "You died for what," he said, and laid his head next to hers.

Rita stared into the sun. The bus had passed its stop, like it often did, and she had chased after. Why was she lying on the ground? Because of her head. Something was in there that wasn't there before, squeezing inside. Other parts hurt as well, left knee, right hand, but the pain in her head was above all else. English words would not do. Only Russian could explain this.

She rolled onto her stomach, to her knees, and looked up at the broken windshield and dented hood, felt the sharp splinters in her hair, the warm blood on her fingers. She stood crookedly, her left leg too short, as if the bones that once met in her knee had passed one another. She reached down and felt her knee, then the ankle, and below. If things weren't bad enough, she'd broken a heel.

"Are you all right?" she said.

Rob looked up at her face. He nodded, thinking, Now I'm dead too.

"Have you seen my heel?"

"Your heel? My God." He looked down at her foot, her broken shoe, then slowly back up to her head. Except for some blood on her hand, she came across as unscathed. Yet he'd killed her. He saw it happen. And now she was alive. He watched her limp toward the car, still looking for her heel. "You're not supposed to be moving," Rob said. He was thinking how nice it felt to lie on the street. "Come over and lie down. It's the best thing for you. I'll call an ambulance. I have a phone. I had a phone."

"I have an appointment at noon. This woman will think I am vagabond like this. I have to find the heel."

"Look at what you did to my car. You can't be walking around."

"I am sorry," Rita said, "it has been a bad week." She stopped her search suddenly, and jerked her head up and back toward the intersection, as if for the first time remembering the crash. "I must go," she stepped over Rob. "My husband will kill if he sees."

Rob looked back to the corner, then at Rita walking up the street. "He'll kill me."

"No, me," she shouted back. "Me."

Rob stood and went to the car, strands of the woman's hair embedded in the glass. The engine was still running, and he put it in drive, following her through the cracks in the windshield, the sun breaking through like a storm washed over. He felt light, suddenly new and clean, like he was the one who'd miraculously survived. He wanted to rush out and kiss her, and write that feeling down. He grabbed the briefcase out of the backseat, found the little tape recorder buried at the bottom that he'd bought months before, hoping it would help him start writing again. He hit the red button marked RECORD:

"A man runs over a woman with his car. He takes her home to care for her. They fall in love. She gets him writing again. She's foreign. European. They have enemies. Their love constantly tested on adventures. Oh God, I've heard this story. Don't worry, Rob. It's going to happen. Be patient. A man runs over a woman with his car. Miraculously, she's fine. She saves him from killing himself. He saves her from a homicidal husband. The accident that brought them together was destiny. They fall in love. Each subsequent episode will star the same two actors, only in different roles, in different parts of the world. The abiding power of love. Love as fate. These two people, no matter where they are, or who they are, are destined to find one another. God that's awful. Keep it rolling, Rob. It's waiting for you."

He stopped the tape player and pulled alongside her. "I'll give you a ride. At least let me do that. I just ran you over."

She looked back up the street, then opened the door and gritted her teeth. "Go up two blocks and make a left."

"I'm sorry I hit you," Rob said, "are you sure you're all right?" He looked over at her small ear that blushed where it had struck the glass, the old red sweater she was wearing, that her shoulders could barely hold up, and that made something tragic of her short black skirt. She pulled down the visor and looked in the mirror, wiping the lipstick from her clenched cheek, less beautiful than the angel he'd seen in the street, yet so real, a woman unstoppable, exactly the kind he'd been born to write. He imagined typing at his desk while she slept in his lap.

"Where are you going?" he asked.

"I am meeting a woman for apartment."

"Look, I was thinking, maybe it's more than just chance, meeting like we did." Rob searched her sweater for a reaction. "Can I buy you lunch or something, we'll get you a new heel. It's the least I can do. What's your name?"

Rita shook her head.

"Come on, just your name? That's not much to ask."

"No, I want to remember," she looked back in the mirror. "But I cannot."

"I'm Rob," he said.

6

Loretta waited outside the blue and gray four-story eight-unit on Haight Street for her twelve o'clock appointment. Everything was ready. The morgue wagon had left with the body, and she'd struck a deal with the super, whom she'd worked with before. He handed over the keys for a twenty, even said he'd hold off the other agents for a day or two. The place was clean enough. But the smell. She found a can of air freshener under the sink. Enough to get her through the interview, if that girl ever decided to show. The dead guy had no family. The apartment came fully furnished.

The cracks in the windshield made the street appear to be sneezing. With his head up close to the glass, his eyes in the space between the two largest lines, Rob could see enough to drive straight. Right turns were a problem. When she told him to pull over, he jumped the curb and struck a lamppost. Her head hit the windshield, this time pushing it out.

"Sorry about that," he said. "I'll just wait for you here."

She stumbled to the sidewalk, her hands holding up her face. "No. Please. I want you to go."

Loretta walked over and put her hand on Rita's arm. "What's wrong, hon?"

"I have to get a place right away," Rita said. "My husband won't leave me alone."

"Believe me I've been there," Loretta said. She couldn't see the driver's face, but she had a clear enough picture in her head. A man who'd drive around in a car like that. Knocks her down the stairs after a few drinks. She remembered the time when Tim tried to hit her, right in front of the kids. So drunk he missed and fell down. Loretta put a chair in his head. "You just let me take care of it. This is the first step of taking back your life. I did it. You're gonna do it too." She grabbed Rita's arm and helped her up the front steps. This poor girl walking with one heel. The scum. "These wounds will heal," she said, "I promise."

"Do you know my name?" Rita asked.

"You're Rita. You work in the bar where my husband Tim is drinking himself to death." This girl had it even worse than Loretta thought.

"I just want a room with sun."

"There's plenty of lamps. It's fully furnished."

Young women and old babies crying in the courtyard. Windows facing north, a brick wall blacked with dirt. The room smelling like air freshener and a dead body. At least the door was strong, three locks. Rita gave the down payment in cash and squeezed her head between her hands as she walked down the stairs, already late for work. The man who'd hit her was still parked outside. She waved before turning up the street, as if to push him away. He waved back.

Loretta walked up to the passenger window and stuck her hair in. "You are going to leave this woman alone," she said. "I know where you live. I know where everyone lives. You lay a hand on her again, and I'll cut your nuts off and shove one up each nose. You get the idea."

"I'm getting it," Rob said. "That woman saved my life." He put the car in drive and stayed half a block behind. His muse, limping on one heel through the cracks in the windshield. Six months without an idea, and now they were pouring in, the energy to live. He hit the record button. "A man runs over a woman with his car. She was escaping from a gang of Russian killers, who continue to beat her even as she lies in the street. The man pulls a gun and sends the thugs running, wounding a few. He puts the woman in the car and drives off. A city of both the future and the past, a disaster zone that seems to belong to another planet—polluted, lawless, insane—Crumbtown. She is beautiful, but wild. Lives by trusting no one. Before he can learn her name, she jumps out of the car and keeps running. He loses her, becomes obsessed with finding her. His name is Exley, a burned-out building inspector. No. His name is Rob, a writer, in a city where all the poets have died. A heart still beats in this heartless place."

Two

SCENE 7

Rita pulled two beers from the cooler and limped over to the end of the bar, one in front of Tim, one in front of Tom. "Now let me get this straight," said Tim. "You say that guy in the suit who is standing right over there in the corner, he hit you with his car this morning and now won't stop following."

"This is correct," Rita said. She bent down and pulled off her heeled shoe and banged it against the bar until the heel broke off.

Tom tilted back in his chair, nodding quietly to his beer, a moment before rocketing forward, pointing the bottle at Rita. "I have a question. Did you go to the hospital?"

"No."

"Did you at least take an ambulance?"

"I'm okay. I keep forgetting my name."

"That happens to me," said Tim.

"Not remembering isn't good enough," Tom said. "You have to be more injured than that. Sometimes it doesn't happen right away, the head, especially the neck," Tom pointed to his cervical brace. "I've been in dozens of accidents, and I'm proud to say I've never been hurt but I've always been injured. And I always take an ambulance. My lawyer says it's very important."

"He's right about the ambulance," Tim said. "It's worth the wait."

"I wish you to go over there and talk to this person, and tell him to leave and go."

"Look, he's wearing a suit, Rita, he's asking you to sue."

"A hit-and-follow," Tom said. "I'm calling an ambulance."

Rita pulled two notebooks from behind the tequilas. One book was titled "Tim," the other "Tom." She placed each before its respective half twin, opening Tom's to flip through the tidy rows of numbers to the last page, in which was written, over ten times, the same phrase—*Do not serve until paid.* "How many beers you had, Tom?"

"Is that my name?"

"Maybe we should talk to the guy," said Tim.

"It's for his own good." Tom removed the neck brace and wrapped it around his empty bottle. "A hit-and-follow."

Rob had been in bars like this. In college in upstate New York, driving through the valleys in Brian Halo's convertible, the roadside lean-tos that wouldn't ask their age, dollar beers and a jukebox in back, the walls bending with photographs, a half century of disasters: blizzards, tornadoes, weddings. Brian Halo regaling the locals, stories about shooting lobsters with shotguns, feeling up cheerleaders in church belfries.

The sign outside said "Gloria's Fine Food and Drink," but the only food Rob could see was a line of potato chip bags hung over a water-stained painting of the sea. Flood was the featured disaster here, floods that seemed to hit this part of the city once a week. Rob looked through the framed newspapers lining the walls, the photos of streets become canals. One showed two men standing in a rowboat as they drank from the bar.

He walked to the back, to a section of photos cut off from the floods. Framed by artificial wooden beams and lit from a small light fixed to the ceiling with tape, the little corner glowed like a cottage shrine. It contained a dozen headlines, the one on the top from 1986, ROBBING HOODS, it read, BANK ROBBERY TURNS INTO RIOT AS MASKED GANG TOSSES $$$ TO CROWD. The photo beneath, apparently from a security camera, showed four men wearing black ski masks, each marked with a white crescent, like a backward C, stretching from their foreheads around to their chins. Next to that was another front page, late December of '87, with big letters. A MERRY ƆHRISTMAS, a photo underneath, of a street littered with red lights and police barricades, ROBIN HOOD GANG TOSSES STOLEN BILLS TO SHOPPERS. There were four more robberies down the wall, the last at the bottom, January 10, 1991, ƆAUGHT, the headline read. ONE DEAD. ANOTHER CAPTURED BY POLICE.

As he bent down to read the caption, Rob realized that he no longer had the corner to himself. Someone had pushed a finger into his back, and left it there, while another had tied one hand like a tourniquet around his arm. "Excuse me," the hand said, "my name is Tim, and this is Tom," turning Rob slowly around. "We represent the bartender whom you ran over with your car. She has agreed not to file suit if you agree to be run over by her car this afternoon."

The man named Tim was built like a soda machine, the other, Tom, like an ice machine. Except for that, Rob thought, they might have been twins.

"Except she doesn't have a car," Tom said dejectedly. He

placed one finger between the ribs in Rob's chest. "And so we've advised her to accept cash."

Rob placed his hands in his pockets and fingered the scattered notes, the suddenly empty threads of his future. He trusted Rita, called her his muse, and like all the others, she returned it with betrayal. He'd been hurt, and was about to be injured. "I don't have much."

"You've got your health," Tim said.

"At least you've got that," Tom bent forward to shove Rob over a table, crying out as he did so, "Oh God, my back."

"I thought it was your neck," Tim asked.

"The neck is the back."

Rob lay on the table for what seemed like minutes. The men grunting as they lifted him to his feet. Tim put his hand on Rob's shoulder, leaning on him for support. Tom's hat fell off. These two had seemed capable enough of beating him up; now Rob was less sure. The man named Tom stood on one foot to get his hat, falling backward as he tried to put it on, the three of them falling into the wall, picture frames crashing to the floor.

"Oh no," said Tim. He lifted the broken frame, the bank robbery photo. "Look what he did."

"What happened?" Tom grabbed the picture. "He broke it?"

Tim grabbed it back, "Look at that." He shoved it under Rob's chin, pointing to one of the masked men. "You see. The crack goes right through me."

"That's you?"

"That's not him," Tom reached over Rob's shoulder. "That's Don, and that's me next to Don, and there's Happy, and that's Tim at the end, the one with the zipper open."

Rob looked over to Rita, then back to the men, the picture in his hand. "You robbed banks?"

Tom reached for Rob's elbow. Rob helped him sit down. "We were heroes," Tom said.

"We were kings," said Tim.

Rob pulled two tens from his pockets, "I work for television," the bills already in Tim's hands, Tim at the bar spreading them flat and neat in front of Rita. "We'll take care of this guy don't worry Rita he won't bother you again."

She poured the drinks and when he was gone she walked to the other side of the bar and poured one for herself, drank it, and filled the glass again, her hand rubbing the lump still growing behind her ear. Like the man who'd brought it, the headache was staying. She knew the vodka wouldn't change that. It wasn't going to fix her shoes, or say her name.

Tom separated two bottles from Tim's crowded fingers. He handed one to Rob, "I was going to write a book about it," he said, "once the statute of limitations was up. Now I just can't find the time."

"Who threw the money in the air? That's a great scene."

"Wait a second," Tom leaned over the table, lifting one shot with his teeth, tossing it back. He wiped his mouth with his hat, "Let me remember."

8

It was ten minutes to closing, but Rita was already done. She sat among the bottles next to the register, her hands holding another drink in front of her. Five men sitting at the bar, all raising their empty glasses, crying, Rita, Rita. She lifted hers and threw back her hair, smiling and swinging her shoeless legs in the air. "That's my name."

"Why did Don do it?" Tom kept asking Rob. He was crying, with one elbow on the table, a cigarette over his head. "We'd hit that bank before. You never rob the same bank twice. I tried to save him. You saw me, Tim."

"I was too busy holding Happy in my arms, he died in my arms, man."

"Happy was a prick," said Tom.

"That's true," said Tim.

Rob turned off the tape player and placed the cassette in his briefcase with the others, more than six hours of recordings he'd have to sift through, a lot of which he couldn't use, the digressions about unfaithful women and loving children, the twins' loving unfaithful father. And a lot of it didn't ring true, Tom punching out the mob boss Maury Threetoes, Tim stealing the boss's car, running over his wife Loretta with it in Atlantic City. He'd work those threads in later, once he sold the pilot, where all the best scenes had to go: the first robberies, the stories of Don Reedy, stories so real they asked to write themselves. Rob thought of all the months he'd wasted in his little room, scratching for every word. You had to go out and find your story, run someone over, get beat up, get drunk, and take a lot of notes. This pile of tapes in his case was already the best thing he'd ever written. Rob was sure of it.

He needed to get some sleep, find a hotel, start putting the pieces together. For the first time in hours he looked up and around the bar, empty except for two men stranded on their stools, the Chinese guy snoring in the corner, and Rita by the register, singing with Al Green on the jukebox. To think that only this morning she was lying in the street, dressed in broken glass, this woman who'd saved his life. Now maybe Rob could save hers. He turned to Tim and Tom. "Don must have had a woman, right?'

Tom giggled and pulled Tim's elbow from under Tim's head. "Oh, you bet, lots of 'em. All kinds. You name it."

"I mean one especially, one who was special."

Tim spoke out of his ear. "That was my problem. Loretta the Terror."

"Don loved everybody," said Tom, "women and men. Not like a queer, though. But one woman." He looked over to Tim. Tim shook his head. "Should there be?"

Rob found his feet and stood on them, his hands still sitting on the table. "There has to be. And there will." He took one step and fell to the floor, Tim and Tom helping him up, the three of them falling to the rail. "Rita," he said, "I want to buy you a drink."

"We are closed," she said, "and I have enough, and so are you."

Rob lifted one eye. "And I'd like to make you famous, if it's not too much trouble."

The front door opened, everyone except Rob turning to see, a man who had to stoop to come in, walking behind the line of men. "How you doing," Rob said, the other men studying their hands.

"Shh," said Tom. "That's Arnold, the owner's son."

Arnold went behind the bar, tearing the money out of the register, counting it while the others sat silently sniffing their fingers. He held up the bills, yelling something foreign to Rita. He pulled her off the counter, pushing her out of his way.

"Hey, what do you think you're doing?" Rob said as the

man passed behind, heading to the door. "Hey you." The man stopped suddenly, checking his pockets like he was forgetting something. He turned around and walked up to Rob and pointed at the ceiling. When Rob looked up, the man stomped on Rob's foot, breaking it. When Rob bent down to scream, the man stuck his knee into Rob's face, breaking that, too.

"Not wise," Tom said when the man had left.

"Very not wise," said Tim, struggling to separate Rob from his fetal position. "I think Tim Barrow could play me. What do you think?"

"Same first name," Tom said. They laid a chair on the floor next to Rob and fit him to it, then slowly raised him up. They stepped back and watched Rob pitch himself to the floor. "We better call an ambulance," Tom said.

"It's always a good idea," said Tim.

Three

SCENE 9

It was the longest sentence Don had ever known, so long it kept him up late, imprisoned his sleep, woke him at four every morning, still going strong at dawn, Don beginning to think it couldn't possibly go on, yet the closer he got to where the end should be, the more the end seemed to grow, and in the end, it was this that finally broke him, almost forty years old, dying in his cell, his life this everending sentence that was, after all, just two words.

Fifteen years. He'd finished ten, but the two humbling parole hearings, and the waiting before each, had turned him into a model prisoner, begging to rehabilitate. His next parole board meeting was three months away, and Don was attending every counseling session and therapy group they gave.

Career planners met each Monday, and dealt with problems the prisoners typically faced in getting and holding a minimum wage job. They asked the men to play out common workplace scenes, each one taking a different role: how to explain a murder conviction in a job interview; how to deal with coworkers who objected to being called "bitch"; how to resolve disputes without the use of choke holds.

On Tuesdays the prisoners' rights committee met with the warden. Don had just been reelected to represent his block, a reward for his role in getting the premium prison dramas included in their cable package. Wednesdays everyone made either coffee mugs or T-shirts, all with the Creosote Correctional logo on the front, a big seller in the Far East and the Midwest. Thursdays the men gathered in small groups to make up stories about their upbringing. Friday was prisoner relations day, in which the inmates were asked to imagine themselves as members of different minority groups.

For the past two weeks Don had been running the Friday sessions for his block, after the regular therapist was hospitalized by Black Nationalists pretending to be Peruvian Marxists. In their last meeting, that afternoon, Don tried to focus the group on the one thing nearly everyone there shared—that each man had his own version of Crumbtown he called home, whether it was a white Crumbtown or a black one. Don had even heard of a Portuguese Crumbtown in Waterville. That's what he wanted to get across to them, that it wasn't a race thing; it wasn't a religion thing; it was a crumb thing.

He thought the last session had gone pretty well, but as soon as the lights went down the screaming started, everyone shouting over one another, at one another, and what they said was always the same, always about blame.

Marion was in the cell to the right, still cursing at the wife he'd killed for kissing Marion's brother the way she did. And Mohammed in the cell next to that, who never stopped talking, all night long how much he hated the Muslims, Allah's secret societies in Ohio. And then there was Don's cell mate, Poppy, shouting from the bunk below, every different way he was going to kill his own father, who was also in prison, the very first day they were both out together.

Don tried not to dwell on what had gotten him into this position; he tried to think of what he'd do when he got out. During the day he looked through travel books of places he wanted to see, the great deserts, the Gobi, Sahara, and Texas. But in the evening, listening to the men and thinking about the long night waiting awake for him, he would wonder if there was anyplace he could go that wasn't where he'd always been.

Don once read that twenty-five percent of all men born in Crumbtown ended up doing time. He'd been to prison four times. Four times twenty-five equaled one hundred percent. He never had a chance. All he had to do was follow the crumbs, from his cell back to the house he was born in, that was now twenty feet under the river. Was it just coincidence that after a heavy rain Crumbtown smelled just like a correctional facility?

The minutes before lockdown were the worst, the yelling so loud Don punched his ears to make it stop. Then the guards started blowing the horn, adding to the madness. Men screaming like they were on fire, the guards hosing them down with gasoline. Don pulled his pillow over his face, talking into it so he wouldn't hear what came next, the gunshots from below, one two three; every night for the last ten years. He rolled over in his bunk, knowing what he would see: his friend Happy Jones lying on the floor that wasn't prison concrete anymore, but green marble, the lobby of a bank, the Dodgeport Savings and Loan. And there was nothing for Don to do but go through it again, the whole robbery right to the end. He was standing in the middle of the bank, waiting for Happy to get up, for the blood to stop coming out of Happy's heart. The security guard turning, running for the door, stopping there to take three shots more before disappearing down the stairs. And Tim and Tom, the twins, his old friends, running out too, not a word to him. Don could have done it then, his gun pointed at their backs, and all he did was yell "Come back." What a fool. He bent next to Happy, trying to lift him, then dragging him across the floor, through the sun coming down out of the high windows, the light almost more than he could remember, like it was the light that turned the bank customers against him, tackling him at the door, one of them an old woman, her perfume smelling like the river. Don saw himself fall, his head pressed against the floor, his arm pushed up over his back. He looked out onto the street, at the twins Tim and Tom driving his car. The security guard sitting in the backseat, waving at Don as they drove away.

Don pulled himself out of his bunk and shoved his arms through the bars, squeezing his head between. "You set me up," he said, the words echoing down the line, picked up by a man at the end. "You set me up," the man said, the others carrying it back, louder each time, until it was Don's turn again.

One of the guards paused for a second in front of his cell, and put his stick into Don's side, and walked on without waiting to see him fall. The guard had only worked there for six months, and it had taken more than a few times to learn how little pressure he needed with the stick, in the right spot, no more than tossing a ball underhand to his son.

Don's cell mate Poppy got up out of the bottom bunk. He lifted Don from the floor and turned and dropped him in the bed, shoving him against the wall before rolling in beside. He squeezed Don's hair and slapped him twice in the head. "It's okay," Poppy said, "you're gonna be okay."

10

Brian Halo was around his desk in two steps, a look of athletic concern running across his face, "Oh Rob, so this is why you've been out for two months." He took Rob's cane, helping him to the seat. "Nobody can tell me anything here. What happened?"

"Research," Rob said. "It's much better since the pins came out."

"You see where it gets you, like I always say. Think forward. Ahead. Ahead. Ahead. Enough." Halo walked back to his chair, giving his suit a second to catch up. He didn't wear the fabric so much as allow it to follow him around. "Let's talk about this script you sent in," lifting the pages from his desk. "You've written a crime show without cops."

Rob leaned into his cane. "Crumbtown is post law enforcement, post Bill of Rights. The people have no protection. That's where Don and his gang come in."

"I don't like that name."

"Don?"

"The name of the show, *Crumbtown,* it's so sad. I hear a title like that and I have to go straight to bed."

"It's where they're from."

"Well I'm from Teaneck. Call it Teaneck then. And to be honest with you, that first bank robbery, just great, but then afterward, when they end up in that bar again, you need a chase in there, send them off somewhere."

"Wait," Rob said.

"And those annoying twins you can't tell apart. We have to do something with them."

"This is a real story."

"Of course it's a real story. It's Robin Hood. It's Robin goes to the 'hood.' And we are currently taking care of the chase scenes, which takes me to my next problem, the romance, this Rita character. Here it is, scene twenty-four: she's running away from the bad husband, the Maury guy with the toes, when Don comes along and hits her with his car, great, and let me say having Rita stuck on the hood like that while he's driving away is so right for this, a chase with romance, but then where's the romance. She hardly says a word the rest of the show. And what's with the accent, she's Polish?"

"Russian."

"Please, Rob, make me like this woman."

"Well she's kind of a hard person to know."

"Oh my God." Brian Halo stood quickly and walked to the wall of glass behind his desk, forty stories over midtown. He hummed to himself briefly, and when he was finished he handed the script to Rob. "Here. I'm not selling this." Halo laughed. His tie laughed.

"You don't like it."

"I don't like . . . because . . . I . . . *love*." He opened his arms to his sides, jogging in place behind the desk. "I'm producing it myself."

The pain in Rob's foot returned suddenly and jumped to his jaw, down his left arm. Worse than not liking *Crumbtown*, Brian Halo liked it too much. His recent forays into producing—three flops in two years—*Angelpaw, D.D.S., Minneapolis.*

"I've already got the lead to play Don."

"Who?"

"Little Eddy."

"You're kidding."

"He's ready to go."

"He's seven years old."

"Twenty-two, Rob, and I think it's time we all grew up." Brian Halo took a TV remote out of his desk and pointed it at the big-screen television in the corner. He pushed a few buttons and a boy appeared, standing in a sitcom living room. The boy, about ten, holds out his hand to a man in a cop uniform, and shouts, "Gimme gimme gimme," pausing for the long laugh track.

"Little Eddy? From *The Two of Us*?"

"One of the most popular TV series in history."

"The white orphan who's adopted by the black cop. Six years on one joke."

"Gimme gimme gimme," Brian sang. He pushed up the volume on the TV, Little Eddy breaking into the Gimme Shuffle, which was how every episode of *The Two of Us* ended, the credits rolling over Eddy dancing, that ridiculous James Brown imitation that Rob conceded he might actually have laughed at the first couple of times he saw it, but that now repulsed him. Brian Halo raised the volume some more and began his own Little Eddy dance, moving around the desk to reach for Rob's arms, "SAY IT ROB."

"No." Rob grabbed his cane and stood, "He can't play Don. He can't play anything. He's Little Eddy. I won't let you do this." Rob limped to the door, reaching for the knob, realizing there was no knob.

"I want you to direct."

Rob returned to his chair, the door opening behind, one of Halo's actresses wheeling in a bucket of champagne. Brian handed him a glass, raising his own. "To *The Real Adventures of Robin Crumb*."

Rob drank. He kind of liked the title.

"Just one thing," Halo said, "Little Eddy wants to meet this Don character, to help him get into the role."

"Don's up in Creosote, a fifteen-year sentence."

Brian Halo walked behind the desk. "I'll call the governor."

In the elevator Rob raised his glass to the mirror. "Gimme," he said, and closed his eyes and saw Rita's face again, as he had that first day, pressed against the windshield. He watched her fly away, and in her place, a thousand bills floating. "Gimme," Rob said, a little louder. He'd use three cameras for that shot of Don throwing the money, and he'd use real money too, and real poor people waiting on the bank line, get an actual riot going on the bank floor. "Gimme," he said, as loud as he could, feeling his bones give with it, the writer disappearing and the director taking his place. Brian Halo would have his romance, Little Eddy and Rita. It didn't make a difference. He was directing again, that's what counted. He finished his glass and twisted his lips, pushing out his tongue, the champagne doing its work, even though it wasn't real champagne, just seltzer with a little white wine coloring.

Four

SCENE 11

It was one of those days when the earth was so perfectly pitched that the sun came into the bar at a slower speed than usual, and slowed further as it crossed the line of men, to the point where Tim could see its approach the last six feet, to alight upon his bottle, to bless the beer inside. He'd just heard from his lawyer, his lawsuit about to be settled. The man who'd parked his car on Tim's leg two years ago, while Tim had been napping by the curb, was finally paying up, twelve thousand dollars. If only the man had parked more on Tim's head, the lawyer said, they might have gotten the two million they asked.

The injury itself had actually healed within weeks of the accident, but while limping for so long in support of his case, favoring the ankle run over, he'd ruined what was once a fine knee, the pain requiring ever more alcohol to contain. This day, however, this Monday or Tuesday, he'd stood without ache, almost forgot the cane by the chair that had been his bed, and the first quart he usually gave to his knee, was spent on the lawyer's news instead.

He wouldn't see a cent from the settlement. What the lawyer didn't steal, Loretta got the judge to get under lien, for child support and mortgage payments, designer panty hose and an Eltra convertible. Let her have it all, Tim reasoned, striking the bar with his cane. Let her rent the entire city to the Russians and Chinese. The money didn't matter anyway. Not anymore. Was it Wednesday?

Tim had just found out he was going to be rich, he and his brother Tom, richer than if they'd been killed by a car, or even paralyzed. Brian Halo Productions was about to start shooting their show, *The Real Adventures of Robin Crumb,* to be written and directed by Robert Landetta, and based on a story by Tim and Tom. This last part was still a matter of contention, at least to Brian Halo's production manager, Miss Delouise. She'd offered them a consulting position at five thousand per, but had refused to discuss the life rights to the story, the real money, and hadn't taken their calls in three days. Tom wanted to avoid the lawyers if they could help it, Tim was with him on this, but if Miss Delouise didn't pick up that phone soon, she'd be getting another call, from Quibblebee and Fecklewitz, the assassins from 1-800-SHYSTER.

He finished his fourth beer and went out for a walk, to talk over some more numbers with his brother. Tom wanted to ask for half a million. Tim reasoned they were worth more. If the rights to his ankle cost twelve thousand, what were the rights to his life? He had two ankles, only one life, but a man's life, if measured only in size, was over one hundred times an ankle, not to mention that a man could live without an ankle, but an ankle wouldn't last long without a man—six hundred thousand was a conservative estimate for himself, another four hundred thousand for Tom—he was smaller than Tim—made an even one million. If they were worth one million, Tim reasoned, they should ask for five.

He made a right onto Low and took it over to Van Brunt, trying to guess where *Ten Thirteen* was shooting that day. Tom worked part time for the show, parking cars. Tim had worked part time there too, he'd worked part time for every show shot in Crumbtown, and had been fired from each, drunkenness, mostly, and napping on the curb. The production manager for *Ten Thirteen* found Tim sleeping in Dyan Swaine's trailer one day, and had his actors throw Tim off the set. Which was ridiculous; she'd practically invited him in on several occasions, one of the five most beautiful women on television. He'd given her cigarettes when she was trying to quit.

He made a right onto Dyre, and three blocks later he found the principal actors' trailers camped in a line down Delinquency. Tim stayed in the street, along the backs of the trailers, until he got to hers, the second biggest on the set. He pulled himself to the little window, the space in the curtain, Dyan in her blue bathrobe, Tim's favorite.

He knocked on the glass with his forehead, "Dyan, it's Tim," his fingers slipping off, clawing back up. "They're making a show about me and I want you to be in. You'd be so perfect to play my wife Loretta."

Dyan held up her hand. The curtain closed.

"I'll come around front," Tim said. He had to get down from the window anyway, his fingertips were about to break off, and there was a car pulling up, security. Tim dropped to the street and tried to crawl under the trailer, the sound of the car door slamming. Anthony King pulled him out by his legs. "What did I say?" King said, before kicking Tim hard and grabbing his shirt, shoving him up the street. "What did I say," he said again, and ran back to the car and got in and drove up to where Tim had fallen, kicking him again, "I was going to do to you if I caught you here again?"

Tim remembered when King was a ten-year-old fat kid who used to park Maury's cars for a dollar. Now he was head of *Ten Thirteen* security, driving a new Fort Worth, wearing that ridiculous eye patch when he could see perfectly. Tim raised his cane while limping away, "You better watch out," he said, "I've got my own show now." King went back to the car and revved the engine, just loud enough to make Tim fall down. Then he grabbed some towels from the backseat and began mopping up the latte that spilled when he was braking.

12

Dyan Swaine closed the curtains and continued her pacing, back and forth in the tiny trailer she'd been given. "They're killing me, Brian Halo," she said, "going to shoot me in the street like I'm a criminal or something."

Brian Halo sat respectfully in his suit, sipping tea in a chair of plastic wood. "This is the news that I heard," lowering his eyes to each side. "That's why I came."

"It's all right there," she pushed the script across the table. "Scene thirty-seven. Captain Palmer runs from the store. The terrorists shoot. She's hit in the back. A lot of blood. She sinks to her knees. Captain Palmer dies."

Brian Halo covered his eyes. "I can't understand. They're doing this because of money?"

Dyan walked to the door-sized mirror next to the sink, and with a fistful of tissues wiped a mole off her cheek. "It's not about the money," she said, "it's about half a million dollars, the same amount they're paying Lieutenant Gates. That's all I ever asked for, equal pay."

"You're worth more, Dyan."

"I know, right, I'm the captain. He's just a lieutenant. I've got sixteen web sites. But it's not about the money and I told them that, just pay me the same as him and I'll come back, and what's their answer, they have me kidnapped." She grabbed a blue towel from the rack and wrapped it around her head, pushing under the loose strands of blond hair. "For two months they have me tied up in the back of this little store. That terrorist gang I busted last year. It's so humiliating."

"They're animals," Halo said, "you deserve better." He opened his briefcase and took out a script, Dyan pulling it close so she wouldn't have to squint, the wrinkles under her eyes that started last winter, the day she turned thirty. "It's not a cop show, is it? I'm sick of cops."

"It's a Robin Hood story, about these bank robbers who give away their money."

She went back to the sink, bending over to brush her teeth. "I want to rob banks," she said. "I want to give to the poor."

"You play the Maid Marian character. Rita. She's smart, she's beautiful . . ."

"Don't tell me that," she spit. "Tell me I'm Rita Hood. Tell me I do everything he does." She rinsed and spit and brushed some more, her teeth that were always too big. "Who is he?"

"Who?"

"Who's Robin Hood?"

"You're going to love him."

"Who?"

13

Ava unlocked the door and pushed it open with her shoulder, and felt for the light. No light. "Eddy?" she whispered, flicking the switch down and up. "Eddy? Come and get it, Little Eddy." She opened the door further, stepping into the apartment, saying to the dark, "The light's out," then screaming when something pulled at her arm. The door closing. A gun pushing against her cheek, pushing her inside, down the two short steps to the living room.

"Don't you move or make a noise," a voice said. "I'm here to help. Got it. But if you scream, I'll blow your head off. Okay."

She took one of the man's fingers into her mouth and bit down, hard enough for him to yell. She found the lamp and turned it on. "Eddy, you scared me."

"Pretty good, huh." He put the gun on the table and grabbed her pocketbook and turned it over, shaking out everything.

"Don't do that. Justwaitaminute." She grabbed her purse. "And listen to me, nobody puts the gun against somebody's cheek like that. What are you going to do, blow my teeth off?"

"It would hurt. You got to admit, and don't call me Eddy. Call me Don, like the character." He frantically separated the items on the table into plastic, metal, and paper. "All right, where is it?"

"I mean it, Eddy. If you're gonna act like a guy who robs banks you got to know these things." She took off her jacket and draped it over Eddy's head, watching him as he blindly searched through the pockets. "Are you hearing this?"

One of his hands went through the lining, up to his elbow in the pocket. "Okay, where is it?"

"Oh Jesus, Eddy, what are you doing? You gotta just take a second and look at yourself here. Gimme gimme gimme."

Eddy threw the jacket at the kitchen and sat down and slapped the couch. "What did I say about that."

"Ah baby, I'm sorry." She came back with the jacket. "I didn't mean to say that. Here you go." She pulled out a piece of foil the size and shape of her eye and spread it open across the scraped glass of the table. "Is that better, Little Donny?"

He grabbed one of the blunt razor blades by the dictionary. "All that technical shit with the gun can wait," he said. "Everybody's got their own way of doing things. That's why I got to know Don's head first, got to get it right up here, inside, then you know how he holds his gun." Eddy sawed the powder into thin lines, measuring each with his middle finger. "You know they're getting him out of prison just to talk to me, to help me with the role, but I gotta be ready for that, I gotta already know how I'm going to play him before I meet him. Because seeing the real person can really throw you off sometimes. Like maybe he's different now, prison changes people, who knows, maybe it ain't even him anymore. Or maybe he's playing a part too, that he wants people to see, or he's trying to be who he thinks I want him to be. That happens all the time. It's why I need to concentrate. It's all I've been thinking about."

She laughed with her head bent back over the chair, "Oh, that's all you were thinking when I was out."

"Yeah, and you know what?" Eddy let the straw dangle out of his nose one second before applying it to the glass. "I think this guy likes to do coke."

14

Since seeing the warden that evening, Don had done little more than roll in his bed, pretending sleep, through mealtime and the riots of lights-out, rolling over what the warden had told him: a parole from the governor. Freedom in the morning.

He couldn't stay in his bunk any longer; he needed to get up, take a walk to clear his head, three steps up, three steps back. If it wasn't for his cell mate Poppy, all the questions, everything that would have to be said. Slowly Don moved toward the edge, waiting for the sounds of his cell mate's breathing, the sinister rhythms of Poppy dreaming. When Don was sure it was asleep, he peered over the side, Poppy's eyes open wide.

"It's awake, *sí*, but does it talk," Poppy pulled himself up, head bent against the top bunk, always speaking out of a bald spot. "You gonna tell me now what this is."

"I got parole."

"What?"

"I'm getting out in the morning, couple hours."

"Your hearing's next month. You can't talk to me?"

"It's not parole exactly. It's TV."

"You got TB?"

"Television, Poppy. They're making a show about robbing banks. I'm supposed to be a consultant."

"Shit, I heard about this. What happened to Witherspoon. You know him. Same thing."

"Car's picking me up at seven."

"Same thing, man. Car picks him up. Then like one month later, send him back."

"I'm not coming back."

"I know that. I don't want you to go. Okay. TV people."

"They sent him back?"

"Oh yeah, man, he had that lisp, you know, his teeth sticking all out, they wanted a safecracker man but not one lookin' like that." Poppy bent down and punched the bed. "This happenin' too fast. Supposed to be next month. What am I gonna do? Ow, shit. Come here."

Don lowered himself to the floor, Poppy's half of the cell. "They say I got to stay in Crumbtown until the show's over." He sat on the far end, the mail-order pillows from Puerto Vallarta. "What if it's never over?"

"You got to be there anyway, right, take care of the business."

"I'm on parole, Poppy, I can't just start shooting people."

Poppy punched himself in the chest. "They ran on you man, those twins, you never let go of that. It's what keeps you strong. Twenty-five years I'm strong." He punched himself again. "Why they making a show 'bout you. Should be making the Poppy show." He stood and punched the wall. "Don't you come back. You hear me. You never come back. I'll kill you if you do." He sat on the bunk and wrapped his arm over Don. "I don't want you to go."

15

Loretta parked behind the morgue truck and walked down the well-lit path to 43 Holly, an Upper Dodgeport prewar that she'd kill to live in, apartments the size of tennis courts, lawyers and doctors and television anchors. She'd yet to sell a listing up here, too high on the hill for her clientele, but that didn't stop her from getting out of bed in the dark, the red lights of four o'clock. For herself she did this, and for the kids, the day when she crossed that bridge for the last time, the new office she was going to open. This was the Loretta that was moving here, taking with her only two daughters and a mink coat. One of those new buildings on the slope, a doorman that said yes ma'am, who'd never let in the kind of person she'd been, the Loretta who had married Tim.

She'd hire someone to work the Crumbtown office, the steady commissions of Russians and Chinese. Her new place she'd start on a street like this, or one of those little garden lanes off Washington, walking distance to the old factories by the station that were being turned into condominiums. The changes happening so quickly, every time she crossed the bridge she noticed. Big money moving in, legitimate companies, insurance and advertising, the Internet kids from New York—you'd have to be an idiot not to rake it in.

But money alone did not mean success, all the investment shows she watched, they kept getting that wrong, you didn't just write a check to become a new person, pretend like yesterday never happened. What would a new house do for her, a new car, if she was still getting late night calls from the bar. Talking to clients with Tim banging on the window, asking for another loan. How helpful would the doorman be with Tim standing outside her building, crying her name for every neighbor to hear. Nine years of this, kicking him out, then letting him back, enough times to know—the past could not be forgotten, only cut off.

She stood at the entrance, ten names in a stainless frame; Harry forgot to tell her what apartment. A suicide was all he said, a divorcé, laid off, alone. She looked up at the windows, no lights, so she went down the list, the Greenes and Greenbaums and Kims, searching for the most likely candidate—Fitzgerald, 5A—about to push the bell when the horn started, a blue Meteor parked across the street, the big man inside. He'd been watching her all this time.

Detective Hammamann leaned over and opened the passenger door. "They'll be done in a few minutes." He patted the seat, "Come on sit down Loretta it's cold out."

Harry hadn't forgotten to tell her the apartment. He wanted this scene, watching her at the door, honking across the street. She'd never seen him in a Meteor, had to add that to her list, the cars he followed her around with, the disguises he wore, the love letters he managed to deliver without her seeing, in her pocketbook, a dresser drawer, the windshield on her car. She liked this about him, the preparation he brought to a relationship. It was the follow-through she had problems with. Every man she met. She wasn't getting in. "Which apartment Harry?"

"Come on Loretta," he pushed the door open further. "I want to tell you something."

"My ears are working."

He looked left, then right, "What we talked about," his voice dropping. "About Tim. I've taken care of it."

She stood on her toes and grabbed for the door handle, trying not to shout, "You did it?"

"Tomorrow," he said.

"Oh no," she closed the door.

"It's all set. I promise. Loretta. Look. There's something else I want to show you." He pulled a blotted slip of blue paper from his jacket, pushing it through the half-open window. "It's the suicide note, from the guy in 5A, a hanging. I found this in his pocket. You wanna read?"

"5A," she said, "That's what I was gonna guess." She reached for it. He pulled back. She crouched next to the door, her mouth on the top lip of the window. "Come on Harry let me see."

He handed over the note, watching her open it, her eyes recognizing the script, the wide square capitals, Harry's writing, another love letter. DEAR LORETTA, she read. He'd set her up again. I CAN'T LIVE WITHOUT YOU.

Harry smiled, "It's true."

She opened the door, sitting next to him in the car, his arm around her neck, "Oh Harry," she said.

ACT II

Five

SCENE 16

Don signed more forms in the little gray office by the front gate for the release of his wallet and clothes, the free key ring and personal organizer. Then the guard pushed a red button and the gate slid apart to expose the small parking lot, empty except for a spindly maple shoved against the far edge, a man in brown aviators standing in its shade. The man held up a white board with the name "D Reedy" printed on the front. Don covered the sun with his hand, watching a car pass on the road behind the lot, the low ridge in back blanketed with new dirt, a bulldozer sleeping on the top. The man raised the sign high and waved it over his head, like he was standing in a crowd of much taller men. "Go on," the guard said.

His driver wore sandals with black socks, a batting glove on his left hand. "Let's get out of this sun before it kills us. Ha," he opened the back door of a black 10,000VTLr and pulled onto the main road that was mostly gravel. He kept pushing buttons to make the fan go louder. "There's a binder next to you, with a white envelope clipped to the front. Open that."

Don pulled out the five twenties that were in the envelope. He looked in the binder; it held half a dozen folders: "A Halo for the 21st Century," "Friends of Halo," "Parole Guidelines."

"Don't tell me how much is in there," the man said. He drove for a few miles, quietly reflecting in the rear mirror. "Come on, really, how much?"

"A hundred dollars," Don replied.

The driver turned around to look at Don, then went back to studying him in the mirror. "Yeah, right, who the hell am I."

"Ten thousand," Don said.

"I knew it. Goddamn. I knew it."

Don put the twenties in his pocket and read the opening lines of his parole guide, a brief overview of the television and motion picture industry's early release program that since 1998 had helped over two hundred men and women, and in that time had become a model of prisoner rehabilitation. He pulled out another folder, which held the copy of his contract with Halo Productions. In language generally vague, then suddenly precise, Don had, in exchange for his early probation, forfeited all current and future rights to any representations of his life, both fictional and otherwise. He put the folders back into the envelope and stared out over the watery edge of the highway, the service roads spilling around islands of green and gray, houses crouching above their basements.

They stopped for breakfast at a diner in New Morgan, the inside looking exactly like the out. The driver led him to a booth in the back, Don staring at the menu for five minutes. It had been so long since he had to choose what to eat, and when the waiter came he still didn't know, eggs or pancakes. The driver ordered a fruit salad and pulled out the magazine he'd brought in, which had something to do with raising pigeons. At the table next to Don a woman was watching talk shows on a handheld television. She wore headphones, but with the volume so high, it sounded like dogs fighting. The other tables around him were full of people who'd ordered the wrong things, and the waiter kept coming back, three times, and finally Don just ordered the eggs, scrambled, and when they came they tasted just like prison. He poured ketchup over everything anyway. Everybody knew where he'd been.

He was asleep before they hit Waterville, and an hour later the driver woke him at the hotel, the door opening onto a sidewalk of fake grass, which led to a lobby of cracked stucco and pink glass, a young woman talking to her computer at the front desk. She handed him a card she called a key and said the minibar and pool were not available to parolees. When Don finally figured out how to get into his room, he double-locked the door and sifted through the pamphlets on the desk, credit card applications, and guides to nearby riverboat gambling.

Someone was knocking. He went to open the locks, and the phone started to ring. While the phone rang, the man at the door handed him a package. Don brought it to the bed and answered the phone. A Miss Delouise, from Brian Halo's office, told him she would be serving as both his production manager and his probation officer. She asked him to open the package. Inside was a portable phone no bigger than Don's ear. It came with an instruction booklet the size of the Bible in his desk. Ms. Delouise called it a cell phone, and said that it would replace his prison cell. Don and the cell phone he was holding must never part, she said. Don was responsible for maintaining battery charge and remaining within high-reception fields. Two missed calls was considered a violation, and would require Halo Productions to notify the police, where a Detective Harry Hammamann was liaison.

Don opened the instruction booklet, but before he finished "How to Turn On Your Phone," the little thing began to ring.

He pushed a few buttons but the ringing continued. Then the big phone next to the bed joined in, hi-lo, hi-lo, like a police siren. Someone was back at the door, knock knock, politely at first, then louder. He pushed some more buttons, the phones getting louder with every knock. Don backed into the wall, beneath the striped paper, the familiar smell of concrete. He pushed more buttons on the phone, yelling at the door, "Wait a second." He went to the window by the desk, ten floors to the street; he jumped on the bed. "Come in," he said, and when the young man from the flower shop entered, Don rushed the opening, pushing past the man's bouquet, out the door, Don taking the stairs. A little card falling to the floor: *Compliments of Brian Halo.*

17

Brian Halo stood at the eastern edge of his office and looked out at the skyline fused white by the sun. Rob walked in quietly and took a seat facing the window, the light pounding him through the glass, and waited for Brian Halo to turn around. It was nine-thirty in the morning, and Rob was about to be fired.

"For weeks I've dealt with your excuses," Halo said to the window. "Then this," he raised the script and at the same time lowered his head, like a preacher holding a vandalized Bible. "This, Rob," he turned slowly, his shadow thinning, then getting wider until it covered the desk and chair, "is why I love you."

Relief hit Rob so hard it nearly knocked him off the chair. He squeezed his legs to force out the air. "I thought for sure you were going to fire me."

"You're my director and my friend, why I asked you to come in. We're going to make it work."

Brian Halo's shadow moved to the left, Rob strained his neck to stay in. "You like it. I'm so glad. I was having some trouble there with the Rita character, but yeah it is pretty good."

"No, it's not good at all," Halo sat down, "it's terrible, so much worse than before. Now she's unconscious for the entire second act, and then just before she wakes up you had the bright idea of having Don gag her and tie her to a chair."

"Because he cares about her."

Brian Halo reached across the desk, grabbing Rob's knee. "We're not going to argue, okay, because the actress who is playing Rita loves the story, and I love this actress, which is why I love this story too. Are you ready? Miss Dyan Swaine herself is playing Rita."

"She's *Ten Thirteen*."

"Not after Saturday. Contract's up. The captain's getting shot."

Rob crossed his legs; he slapped his lap. "Wow. So Dyan Swaine likes the script."

Brian Halo pulled some papers from a drawer. "She likes the story, Rob, and some of the script, she says, is not awful. Here, she faxed these over, just some ideas, okay? You can fill in the dialogue. She wants to write this with you." Brian Halo was around his desk, holding Rob's hands. "It's all coming together now. Let it come together." He let go and walked to the window, turning into the sun. The meeting was done.

18

Don ran down the stairs through the lobby to the doors to the street, pushing buttons on the phone until it stopped ringing, the screen at the top stopped blinking, "1 missed call," it read. He looked up the block, the offices emptying for lunch, cars and trucks driving past, places to go. He checked his phone again and made a right, took three steps and turned, back three steps and turned. Ten years. He leaned forward, almost to the point of falling, putting his foot out at the last second, and another, like he was going down a steep hill.

The old industrial section had been cleaned up, the brick factories converted into factory outlets, their first floors shining with new sneakers and bath oils and wine-tasting equipment. This area that used to look just like Crumbtown, only without the floods. Now the sidewalks were straight, the streetlamps new, every other one with a flag that said "Old Dodgeport" on it. Down on Front Street the bus terminal had been turned into a performance space, and next to that, a new glass tower where the ironing offices used to be. He passed two cranes over an empty lot on Beard, and two more over the old dump between the station and the interstate. Signs on the wall said it would soon be forty stories of new gambling. Don turned under the highway, three blocks then left on Washington, the view down two miles to Crumbtown, looking the same as ever, patched roofs, streets angling into the water.

He pulled out his phone and checked it again, the wind hitting him with the first smells, salt water and coal smoke, and somewhere close by, a donut shop. He raised his eyes to the sun, staring straight in, warmed by the glare. In prison, the sky took all the color out of you, but out here you took it back, new cars and restaurants, girls in dresses. This time was going to be different.

He stopped at a new pizza place on the corner, Old Dodgeport Pizza, and stood at the counter, wondering what to order—ten years he'd been thinking about it. For several minutes he stared at the aging slices, which looked like they'd been made in a warehouse, the men at the oven who were too skinny to know good pizza. Don turned around and walked out; he'd waited this long, he could wait twenty blocks more, down to Crumbtown, to the world-famous Coliseum, the best pizza in the city. And the only way to get it was to cross that bridge, because the Coliseum didn't deliver. Sometimes, when you lived there, that pizza made up for everything.

Down the hill almost running, he took off his jacket, rolled up his sleeves, the sun on his arms, breathing too quick. The Coliseum, since 1936. He'd sit at his old table, watch the girls walk through, maybe talk to a few. What had he been thinking in prison? That he wanted to go live in the desert? End up watching TV all day, watching other people live. Frozen pizza that tasted like scrambled eggs.

He crossed the bridge into Lemmings, the familiar horns and derision, just like he remembered, jealous and drunk and mean-looking, except that the stores had changed names and all the people looked Chinese. Sally's Pawnshop was now a tailor who did acupuncture; Jamie's Liquors was run by a barber who sold exotic birds and umbrellas. Don had always wanted a parrot, and he stood a long time looking at one in the window, but the tag said three hundred dollars, and the bird looked sick and he hadn't just walked three miles to look at parrots. He stayed on Lemmings, two more blocks to Leak, and turned the corner and stopped, and looked back, checking the signs; he knew where he stood—Coliseum Pizza was now Secret Ocean Fish.

Buckets of live crabs in the window, eels and squid and creatures he'd never seen before, some longer than his arm, stretched over beds of white ice, staring at him like they wanted to fight.

He walked back to Lemmings, his hands in his pockets, looking left up the hill, then right, to Gloria's bar, two blocks below, its awning stripped and twisted that way since the hurricane came through. The bar had always been named after storms named after women.

He walked faster into the street, nearly hit by a car as he started to run, heading for the bar. He wasn't looking to start anything, if the twins were there, just ask a few questions, about loyalty and friendship and why Tim and Tom would be leaving a bank robbery with a security guard in their car. Maybe they had some questions for him. That'd be fine too. Get it over with. Don stopped at an alleyway, an old wooden table someone had thrown away, two legs still attached. He broke one free, solid and not too long. Swinging it at the air as he ran, liking the weight.

Two painters were working in front, scraping Gloria's name off the window. Don chased them away with the leg he was waving, "What's going on?" He put his back to the door and rested there a moment until his breathing slowed, his lungs out of shape. Maybe the hotel had a gym, maybe a separate section where the parolees could work out. He pressed his nose against the glass, his hand over his eyes as he looked inside. The bar was covered with cloth. Two more painters working behind it, also covered in cloth, covering the walls.

On the table closest to the window was a computer and phone bank, more computer equipment against the wall. So Gloria's was gone too.

He threw the table leg up the street, head bent to his chest as he passed the bar. You are on parole, he said to himself. Slow down. Breathing in deeply, he buttoned his jacket, combing his hair with his fingers. Enjoy yourself. The next two blocks were the same ones he knew, warehouses that had been falling down since Don was born, the half-shuttered store at the corner, that sold only things in pieces. But the scene changed as soon as he crossed Delinquency. Suddenly the sidewalks were level, the power lines gone. It looked more like the Lemmings of the seventies, with curtains in the windows, signs over the stores. A barbershop with a real barber pole, a candy store that looked like it sold more than betting sheets, and next to that, a beautiful sign in white script, *Sal's Neapolitan Fountain.* Don was going to have some pizza after all.

Except where were the people? Something was wrong. Then he saw what, two patrol cars coming up the street, parking right in front of his pizza. A plainclothes cop got out of the first, bald, with a black patch over one eye, two uniforms stepping out of the other, standing behind. The plainclothes looked at him strangely, probably that eye patch the guy was wearing, and pulled out a walkie-talkie and began speaking into it. Don smelled a major police operation under way. Be cool, he said to himself, no crime in getting a slice. He walked past them, catching the light blue letters on the car, NYPD. An operation so big they had to call in New York.

Sal's Neapolitan was locked. He pulled on the door twice more and looked in the window, piles of boxes filled with framed pictures. And nothing to do but pass the cops again.

He nodded slightly to them, five eyes staring back. Then the phone in his pocket started to ring, right on time. He pulled it out and coolly dropped it on the sidewalk, and picked it up, poking the buttons until the ringing stopped. No one was talking. The little screen read "2 missed calls." A violation.

"Hey Don," said one of the cops behind him, the plainclothes with the patch. "That's you, right?"

Be cool, Don said, go see what he wants, but instead he found himself walking away, and walking too fast. "Where you going?" the voice getting louder. "Stop."

Don't run, Don said, do not run, then the sirens hit him from behind. He was running. Half a block up another plainclothes, wearing a headset with a microphone, stepped out of a stairway and pointed at Don, yelling "I got him. I got him. Stop. You can't go through." Don put his shoulder in the man's chest, knocking him to the ground. He made the corner without breaking stride, the cop cars gaining from behind. Up ahead, two more sirens coming at him. A big crowd of people on his right, forty or more, huddled like they were handcuffed together. He heard the cop car braking behind him, and felt his legs going up, his head down. He hit the windshield and rolled left and onto the ground, coming to a stop before a storefront. He got up and ran through the door.

"Who are you?" asked the man behind the counter. He wore a long beard, a white turban.

Don looked out the window, more patrol cars pulling up. He ran to the back of the store, found an open door to a little room where a cop was gagged and tied to a chair, a really pretty blond female captain cop, another man in a turban standing over her with a pistol. This is bad, Don said, and elbowed the man in the nose, grabbing the gun at the same time, the man folding into the captain's lap. He ran back to the front of the store, and watched at least ten cops get out of their cars and crouch down with guns drawn.

"Hey dude," said the bearded man behind the counter. "Are you supposed to be here?"

"I'm not going back," Don said.

"In that case, you better get down," the man pulled an assault rifle from somewhere under the register and pointed it at the cops.

Don raised his gun, wondering who to shoot, realizing he couldn't shoot. The gun wasn't real. It was lighter than his hand, just a toy painted black. Don could tell the assault rifle the man held was a fake too. These crazy Muslims or Hindus or whoever they were, were fighting cops with fake guns. He backed into a rack of breath fresheners, knocking many of them with him to the floor.

"Cut, that's a cut," the man with the turban called out, and placed his rifle under the counter. Don shoved the toy pistol under his belt. The plainclothes cop came in, the one with the headset, whom Don had knocked over on the corner. "What the hell. Somebody tell me." He bent over Don, inhaling furiously. "What the hell were you doing?"

Don slowly unwrapped a piece of gum from the floor and chewed contemplatively, to cover up the fact that he'd lost his breath, and that it wasn't coming back. The guns were plastic. The cops were actors. Television. Maybe this was his show, *The Real Adventures of Robin Crumb,* although he'd never kidnapped a police captain or worn a turban. "I was jogging," he said.

The second man with the turban came out of the back room holding a towel to his nose. "Should I untie the stand-in?"

"No," said the man with the headset. "We're going right away. And I need security in here. All right everybody, let's go, back to first positions."

Don pointed to the young man's shoe, which was stepping on the already stained cuff of Don's ten-year-old trousers. When the man didn't move, Don lifted the shoe with his hand. He took the gum out of his mouth and placed it on the ground. He placed the shoe on top of it.

"Oh that's too much." The man with the eye patch had come in, whom Don had seen at the pizza place and thought was an undercover cop. "Hey Don," the man laughed, "how you doing?" Don remembered him then, Anthony King, the fat kid who used to run numbers for Maury.

King reached down and pulled him up. "I thought you were in Creosote. We better get you out of here before everybody's stuck to the floor."

They walked out of the store and up the street, cops running past them to get back in their cars, reversing at high speed to the corner, back from where they'd come. King grabbed Don's arm, "Let's go," he said, "I'm head of security here. I got to make it look like I'm throwing you off the set."

Don shook his arm free. "What show is this?"

"*Ten Thirteen*. You must have just got out, am I right. That suit you got on."

"I'm supposed to be on *The Real Adventures of Robin Crumb*."

"The bank robbery thing. Where Dyan's going. That's your show?"

Don nodded, "TV parole."

"That's how I started." King stopped at the corner, pulling Don back, more cop cars reversing past. "They got me out to consult on this informer character who ended up being cut after two episodes, but by then I got my hand in too many places for them to send me back. Now I'm working security, driving Dyan at night, do some acting on my days off. You got to keep the cash flow going to pay off the man, Detective Hammamann. You remember him, right, probably be calling on you pretty soon."

"How much does he get?"

"Fifty a day, plus you got to listen to his shit, he'll talk your ear off, I can't stand that."

A voice on King's walkie-talkie screamed "Rolling," and from up the street the sirens started. "Come on," King put his arm around Don's shoulders, steering him around the corner as the voice on his radio screamed "Action," the cop cars skidding by.

"I missed a couple of calls," Don said.

"Oh man, you missing calls. I don't know what Hammamann charges for that. That's why I'm saying you got to stay ahead. The key word in this business is action, not reaction. Like when you started running back there, total reaction. I'm not even charging you for this information."

King had two earrings in his left nostril and a small sword through his eyebrow, and with the shaved head, that eye patch, he looked exactly like what he was, a pimp, a bully, and an informer. They turned onto a street lined with campers, and

King stopped between two. “Now get off my set,” he said, and punched Don hard in the stomach. Don never saw it coming, only leaving, and the need to bend over.

King jumped back, punching at the air. “You feel soft, man. Joint made you a big guppy, huh. I’m the king here; that’s all you need to know, and I’m telling you this right now. Stay the fuck off my set.”

Don straightened himself against the trailer and stared at King, who pulled aside his jacket to show the revolver on his hip, “Be cool,” King said, but Don was already there, one hand on the cylinder, the other pulling out the plastic gun, pushing it into King’s chin. “Action. Reaction,” Don said, pulling the gun out of King’s hand, punching him in the face.

“King, is that you?” The door to the trailer opened, and a woman appeared, another blond police captain, this one wielding a black phone. “Where have you been, King, and what happened to lunch? It’s two o’clock.”

King sat on his knees on the sidewalk. He lifted his head, “I’ll send someone, Dyan,” watching for where Don had pocketed the gun. “One minute.”

She came down the steps, “I have a close-up coming up I’m trying to get ready for, and everybody’s eaten already. My stand-in gets more food than me and she’s tied up all day.”

“All right, Dyan. You don’t worry. Go inside and let me take care of it.”

“Dammit,” she yelled, “I’m not dead yet.” She pointed her phone at his chest. “Now please go do it, and get me a cigarette.”

Don and the woman watched King go. She turned to him, her head coming up to his shoulder, the gold badge on her chest pointing straight at the sun. "You don't smoke, do you?"

"Not yet."

"That's good," she said, and turned back into the trailer, shutting the door behind.

Don pulled out King's gun and checked the clip, and put it in his jacket pocket. Then he pulled out the fake gun. He'd keep that, too, in case he ran into another TV set. He put it in his other pocket, next to the phone. Where was the phone? He'd lost his phone.

Six

SCENE 19

Tim and Tom walked into the Dodgeport Savings and Loan and were quickly met by a cloud of plaster that covered Tom's baldness and gathered in his crevices and made the workers around him look like potbellied ghosts. It was the same bank the gang first robbed in '86, that had been closed since '93 and was now used almost exclusively for TV. In the last eight years Tom had seen at least a dozen robberies filmed there, two loan applications, one deposit. His mother still calling him at the bar every time it came on, saying, "I saw that bank you robbed on the television again."

Through the lobby they followed the handmade signs that said "Production Office," arrows in red marker leading them past the workers to the wide marble staircase and down a long hall to a desk where a receptionist was talking to herself through a white mask. She directed them through the double doors into a large wooden office, air-conditioned to such a degree that Tom thought the plaster on the rug was frost.

"Sit down," Miss Delouise said, "please," spitting out the last word as if it was something too hot. "You wish to speak to me."

Tom sat, then stood. She raised her hand and he sat again.

"You are making a television show about our lives and we have come to insist on our proper dispensation."

"How well put," said Tim.

Miss Delouise blew the dust from a stack of pages on her desk and said, "Okay. Here's the script. Now tell me whom you are supposed to be."

"I'm Tom and this is Tim. We're half twins."

"I'm sorry, but there are neither Toms nor Tims nor twins."

"We were in the gang with Don and Happy, we robbed the banks and gave the money back to the needy and now we need to get paid."

"Hear, hear," said Tim.

"I've got a Don and a Happy here," Delouise said, "and I've got a Renaldo and a Cam."

"Renaldo?" asked Tom.

"Twenty-two years old," Miss Delouise read, "strong, handsome . . ."

"That's me," Tom said.

"Mexican-American," she continued.

"That's Tim," Tom corrected. "What about the other one, Cam?"

"Twenty-one-year-old African-American."

"I'll be Renaldo," said Tom.

"Neither one of you fit these descriptions." She pointed to Tom, "You are middle-aged and fat and balding, and you," she pointed to Tim, "have dandruff and—"

"Hold it right there," Tom said. "That's the oldest trick, Delouise; first you steal the rights to our life, then a little surgery, new names. All right now tell me this, one of these guys punches out the mob boss, Maury Threetoes, am I right?"

"That's scene twenty-three, and I believe it's the Don character who does the punching."

"That's a lie."

"What's a lie?"

"I'm the one who punches out the mob boss."

"You punched out the mob boss?"

Tom and Tim looked at each other; they shook their heads, "You think we'd be sitting here talking to you right now if we punched out Maury Threetoes."

Miss Delouise pointed at Tom. "You didn't."

"It's a story."

"We were pretty drunk that night," said Tim.

Tom reached over and punched his brother in the arm.

Miss Delouise widened her eyes, "I want you both to go home and see if you can tell the difference between the facts of your life and the stories you've made up, and when you do, if you do, whatever you do, do not come back here to see me ever again. The man that the Don character is based on, Don Reedy, has already signed a release for this show. That's all I need."

"Don can't sign; he's in prison," Tom said.

"He signed a release to get an early parole. It's a standard form."

Tom stood and ran to the window; Tim moved to the door. "Don's out?"

"I'll call him in," she picked up her phone.

"No," Tom said, reaching over to push down her hand. "What we're trying to say, Miss Delouise, is that we would like to accept the positions you originally offered us, as consultants."

"That position has been filled. We do, however, have a couple of openings, for parking consultants."

"If you could just give us a little advance, a hundred dollars."

"You can pick it up in petty cash," she said, "once you sign this disclaimer."

20

Rita drank her second coffee in the shower, her head thumping against the water, a police siren passing under. All morning she couldn't sleep, one after the other the sirens by her window. No one told her when she signed the lease she'd be moving to the middle of a television set, that every morning the guns would start firing, the police chasing after. She couldn't walk out her door without a production assistant screaming up, Stop, Hurry, Go back. Rita wanted to go back; she missed her old street that had reminded her of Odessa where she grew up, the smells and voices, a sign on the tailor's door, "Russian Food." She poured her third coffee, dressing in the kitchen so she wouldn't have to think, a black skirt, the red sweater she hadn't washed.

Down the stairs and out the door, more sirens on the corner, her headache again. She walked the other way, forty feet, and stopped suddenly to look across the street, the homeless man sleeping on the steps. She crossed over to him, the blackened face and hands, swollen feet, sock parts and filthy bandages. All the sacrifices she'd made to get to this place, moving her boxes on public buses. Every night for the last two weeks thinking her husband was right behind her, now finding him snoring across from her door.

She looked down on the pajamas she'd bought for his birthday, back in Moscow, that brown color you couldn't get here. He looked so little on the stairs, "Misha," she said, and kicked him in the side. When he didn't move she kicked him again, then walked around the alley entrance to the garbage cans on the sidewalk, finding a table leg somebody dropped there. She picked it up and hit him with it, and hit him again, and despite his cries kept hitting him until she could breathe, "Stop following me," first in English, then the Russian, "leave me alone."

"Rediska," he cried, his arms still covering his face. "What? I am working."

She struck the steps by his neck. "You stay away from where I live."

"Where do you live? I work here."

She lowered the leg. "You work?"

"I lie in the street. Fifty dollars a day. For the TV show."

She climbed over him to sit on the top step, looking across to her building, the old lady on the second floor, who slept in a chair by the window so she wouldn't miss any car crashes or sudden weather changes or beatings of husbands. Rita lowered her face to her lap. "You were never going to kill me."

"It was you who killed me, Rediska."

"They were just the words."

"I want to die with you."

"They don't mean anything."

"I want us to die together. That's why I'm working. It costs five thousand dollars to kill us. I know the man who will do it."

"You should have gone home when we were in Brooklyn, like you said. You should never have followed in the first place."

"You choose the place you want it done, Rediska. I will choose the music."

She bent to Misha's ear, "I don't care anymore. Do you understand? If you come near my house I'll hit you again and I don't need to hire someone." She threw the table leg into the street and walked over it and up the block, Misha yelling after, "You choose the place and I hope you don't choose here. I work in this place. But I would not want to live."

21

Don began his search at the fake pizza shop, Sal's Neapolitan Fountain, hoping the phone had fallen out where he started running, not where he finished—he didn't want to go back into that store again. Miserably, he retraced his steps, dragging his feet behind. He was going to rest once he found it. Take a taxi back to the hotel. Lock the doors and order in. Lie in his bunk and watch some television until things calmed down a bit.

Two blocks on Lemmings and no phone. He reached the corner and looked up, the man with the headphones again, "You can't go through." Don could see now he was just a kid, barely twenty, and scared.

"Look, I don't want to go in. I just want my phone back, which must have dropped out while I was at the store. Just tell someone to go for it and bring it to me."

The kid said something into his microphone, only about two or three words. Don couldn't hear, but he knew that two or three words were not enough to ask for someone to go to the store and look for something. They were more like the number of words you would use to call for help, or for the police. A few seconds later the sirens kicked in.

Don stepped forward, forcing the kid back. "Go ahead. Do what you got to do."

The cars came from all corners. Light blue with NYPD on the doors. They cut off the streets, front and sides, climbing the curbs to block the sidewalks, forcing Don backward. He counted seven cars. Cops running up on foot, one on a horse.

"There you go," Don said, backing up the block. "Okay." They weren't real cops, but they looked real, and after a certain number showed up, what difference did it make. He was on parole, carrying a gun he didn't want to use. He walked away, down the only street open, sidewalks cracking under his feet. Who knew how many more calls he'd missed? In less than six hours, he'd lost his phone and picked up two guns.

He stopped at the corner, waiting for traffic, and noticed a woman standing two feet away, brown hair floating above a red sweater, a high skirt on tight heels. He'd almost missed her, this beautiful woman standing in front of him. She was tall, almost to his nose, her hair curly and thick, slightly blond at the ends, rising and falling where she stood. He'd been running around all morning, when all he wanted to do was eat pizza and look at women, that's all a man should be expected to do his first day out of prison. Especially since it seemed like he was going right back in.

He stepped to her side; she looked younger than he first thought, less than thirty. How old did Don look? A lot more than thirty. He put his hands in his pockets, reaching for something to say. Hello, nice day. Then what? He could tell her all about life in prison, his good friends Marion and Mohammed and Poppy. No, he'd say he was in television. She stepped off the curb. The light was green. He was going to say hello.

22

"Hello?" Rob shook his phone, "Don't put me on hold. I can't hold anymore." His foot pressed to the Eltra's floor, the little engine screaming back, eight-five, ninety. "Dyan Swaine? Is it you? You're breaking up. Hello? You're gone." Rob threw the phone at the windshield, resting his chin on the steering wheel. "I can't work this way." He reached across the seat and picked up the pages Halo had given him, reading again Dyan's list of changes, "Don taps Rita gently with the car. She isn't hurt at all. They talk and go dancing. She joins the gang." A hundred more. He threw the pages at the phone, "Stay in control, Rob," the Crumbtown exit a quarter mile ahead, "you're still the director here." He fought the car onto the ramp.

There were some problems with Rita's character; okay, he was aware of that, and some of those problems were in the writing. Rob couldn't find her voice, basically every time she opened her mouth a cartoon started. He tried moving his office into the bar, to watch her work, the way she talked to the other men, she never talked to him. He went back to the scene where they met. Spent afternoons running it over in his head, Rita's eyes in the windshield, looking at his. In that moment after impact, and just before she became unconscious, something had happened between them, something that Rob understood right away, but that was taking the Rita character much longer to grasp.

He made a right onto Leak, quick rights on Locust and Thorn, back onto Lemmings and past Gloria's bar, the painters putting on the new name, Sherwood's (Halo's idea). They were shooting scenes four, nine, and nineteen there, starting tomorrow afternoon, the robbery rehearsals in the morning, dinner with Little Eddy tonight. That left him three hours today to work on her scenes. He had to move quickly.

He made a left onto Haight, not knowing where he was going until he saw her, two blocks ahead, Rita standing on the curb, that same sweater she had on before, the first time they were together. All the hopes he'd had that day, before the surrendering began, Brian Halo and Little Eddy and Dyan Swaine, the mayor's department of TV, Russian bar owners who wanted to be casting directors, a production designer who covered everything in parachutes. Rita was the last thing left that Rob could call his own. His inspiration. She stepped off the curb, into the street. Just pull up beside her and say hi, hear her voice again, see the scene in his mind, remembering how it happened. I'm sorry I hit you.

She started across, not looking, the red light behind her. He'd go back to the beginning, start from the start. Just tap her, he said, the car picking up speed. Easy, he said, Slow down, pushing the gas accidentally. He wanted the brake. Stop, he shouted, though by then it was too late.

23

She started across and Don stepped into the space that she left, waiting a second to breathe her perfume, so that he smelled the car before he saw it, getting faster as it came at them, a red Eltra that wasn't going to stop, leaving him exactly enough time to reach his arms around her and pull back hard, the car just missing, continuing on. They fell as one, onto the hood of a double-parked Dauphin, some very awkward and accidental hand positions on the way to standing up.

"That was close," he said.

She ironed her sweater with her palms, staring so intently at him he had to stare away. "Yes, very close," she said, and turned to walk up the street. Don lay on the hood for several seconds, watching her go. The hell with the phone. He was going to get her number.

He was halfway across the street when another car came through the light, skidding to a stop in front of him, blocking his way. A gray suit stepped out, holding a gold badge, the same face that had arrested Don ten years before. "Hey Don," Detective Hammamann said. "I was looking for you." He reached into his jacket and pulled out Don's phone. "Guess what I found."

24

Rita had seen the car coming and she was getting out of the way anyway. She hadn't asked for the man's help, she didn't need anyone's help, and she wasn't going to say thank you for what she didn't need. She thought he was Misha at first, grabbing her from behind like that, pulling her down on the hood. And then she thought he was someone else, her old boyfriend, Victor. That moment when they were getting off the car, she had to really look at the man to be sure he wasn't Victor, even though she knew that Victor was dead, at least that's what her mother said.

It was just another example of how little control she had lately over what she was thinking, her head a pile of images and events, no order to it, nothing ever finished. Victor and Misha, the two great loves of her life. Some life. And he didn't look like Victor at all. Now that she had time to think about it, he looked more like that actor whose name she'd forgotten. That's why she was so confused, because for the last few years whenever she would think about Victor, she would always see this actor's face. But now she knew he didn't look like the actor. After seeing this man on the street today, who did look like the actor, and didn't look like Victor at all. She had to admit, she couldn't remember what Victor looked like.

She kept her eyes ahead of her as she walked, a straight line down the middle of the sidewalk. People could get out of her way. They should because she wasn't getting out of theirs. That's the kind of day it was going to be. And she wasn't saying excuse me. Today, they could say it.

She left Odessa in '92. The revolution had begun, that's what the TV was saying, that in Moscow the government was falling, the poets had taken over the city. Victor didn't care about Moscow. No one in Odessa did. A revolution was going on and he just wanted to sit in his little apartment all day drinking wine and listening to his records. The things she could remember so clearly now, the German Charlie Parker poster, the lines on his arm. She was going to design clothes, pants and jackets made out of flags. She wanted him to go. She'd marry one of the poets, she said, if he didn't come with her. A big poet king.

She walked into Gloria's bar and looked at the cloth on the walls, the office equipment scattered around the tables by the window. A young woman now sitting behind the desk in the corner, talking on the rack of phones. Rita brought two beers over to Joe Far and his friend Han. One of the phones rang. The girl at the desk punched a button. "Rob Landetta's office."

Rita looked out the window. It wasn't fair. She could remember the actor's features so clearly. And she hadn't seen that face in years. But Victor could be anyone. She could walk by him in the street and not know it. He was so sick when she left him, he always said he would die, the doctors there were so bad. She wanted that man to be Victor, it made her ashamed to think of it. Rita grabbed a glass and threw it on the floor. Serving drinks in somebody's office.

25

Detective Harry Hammamann showed him the buttons on the phone. "You push this one to talk, this one to turn it off, this gets your messages, this for the sports scores and this for the weather. How much cash did they give you?"

"One hundred," Don searched over the detective's shoulder, the red sweater on Lemmings, still walking, six blocks ahead, maybe seven.

"You give me fifty. The rest I'll take out of your first check, which will be next Friday. I'll forget the missed calls but I got to take out for losing the phone, fifty more. On Friday."

"Okay," Don pushed the bills into Harry's palm. "Okay?" He looked up the street, she was eight blocks away at least. No one could walk that fast. Hammamann grabbed his elbow. "Where are you going?"

The sweater was gone. "I'm going to the hotel. Going to lie down and watch TV." He started up Lemmings, Hammamann staying with him, "No you're not. I know. You're going to Gloria's bar." Don walked faster, Harry right behind him. "Your two old friends are probably there right now, Tim and Tom, or they'll be coming in soon, four at the latest. You'll get yourself into trouble, Don. Don't go." Don started to run, Hammamann running alongside, then slowing, stopping, yelling after. "They ran on you I know, and they're still laughing about it, Don, but you have to forget that, you've got your whole life left to live with this."

Harry waited in the street, eating cashews out of his pocket until Don was out of sight. He had to be careful here, not to push too hard; the best police work was often the most hands off. It was twelve years since Harry moved down from Loudon, a bubble-nosed kid of twenty-six, a seller of vending whose only dream was to get divorced from his wife. In that time he'd learned a few things about police work, the value of remaining in your vehicle, of knowing your limitations every time you get out. Most crimes here were reported before they happened, and it was the officer's primary duty to decide who could be arrested and who couldn't. Unfortunately for Harry, Tim Dwight could never be arrested, not without a significant wave or gesture or nod of the head from Tim's uncle, Mayor Maury, the man who was paying Harry's salary.

He turned the car around, checking the schedule on the dashboard, a left on Sodden, right on Van Brunt, all the way to the water, the China Sub Restaurant. He walked through the alley to the back door, past the steaming limbs of dishwashers, the line of aprons on fire, a blackened archway at the end, Harry peering in to see Loretta at her table, always the same order, her Beef Everything, extra hot. Forty years old and she looked thirty-three, tireless with her hair, the makeup, the knife and fork she worked like a duchess. A real lady, a real estate agent.

She wanted the best chance for them. She'd been hurt too many times. Love was not a gift, she said, that you open and throw away, not like a fishing vacation or a video you rent or a song in your head. It was a sacrifice, and every time he saw her, Harry knew he could pass the test, if it ever came to that. Though how much better for everyone if Don took care of Tim, while Harry was at lunch, or getting his hair cut, far from any killing, that way he could help Loretta with the grieving, start their new life together immediately.

When Chuck the waiter came into the kitchen Harry held up a five-dollar bill and took the bag of fortune cookies from his pocket, last of the batch from his freezer, the funny little fortunes Harry had cooked up: YOU WILL FIND EVERLASTING HAPPINESS WITH A TALL DARK-HAIRED DETECTIVE. He helped Chuck arrange them on the plate and, after a flurry of nods and winks, watched him bring it to Loretta, her thin hands pulling out the paper, reading each, then carefully tearing them into pieces, mashing them with her fork, into her beef. She ate the cookies and raised her hand for the check. Harry walked out the back, praying that Don would take care of Tim, quickly.

26

Don ran as far as he could, about six blocks, until he was standing on a corner, his hands on his sides, searching all directions. The red sweater had disappeared. He stepped back, against a store window, still breathing too fast, glass bending in his ribs.

"Hey buddy," a man said, one of two guys standing in front of him, dressed like painters. "Hey buddy," he said again, pointing at something in the window, "look what you did." Don turned around, the white letters rubbed over the glass, Sheckles Bar, or Shovels or Steel wool, he couldn't tell. He pulled off his coat, white paint dripping off the back. He dropped it on the ground and remembered the guns and pulled the real one out of the pocket, then the phone, shoving them into his suit jacket, looking for an opening to put the fake gun in.

"Don't shoot me," the painter said, backing off the sidewalk. Don waved the gun as they ran up the street, "It's not real." He turned around, seeing himself in the glass. Gloria's bar, a gun in his hand. Like it was all written down. With only one thing missing, two things. He leaned into the window, pressing his hand over his eyes, squinting at the shadows inside. The office equipment was still there, and now a woman was sitting at a desk near the door, talking on the phone. But the bar was open; he could see two men drinking in the far back. Too far to make out their faces. One short, the other tall. It had to be them.

"Okay," he said, still breathing too fast. "Okay." He looked up at the sky, the clouds caught in the web of power lines, lines that were never buried because of the constant flooding. His father used to say the wires were there to keep the buildings from falling back, but to Don they always appeared to be pulling them forward, on top of him. He breathed in deep, he counted to three. "Okay."

The smell he knew immediately, impossible to forget, wet cigarettes and warm beer and something else, too, impossible to remember unless you were in it. He walked past the girl at the desk, his eyes widening to the dark, the bartender with her back to him, blocking his view of the men. He pulled at the gun, first the fake, then the real. The bartender moved to the side, enough for Don to see the two men were Chinese, and definitely not twins. She turned around, three of them staring now. Her face, the girl from the corner.

"Well," Rita said, "the handyman is here." She'd changed her red sweater for a tight white shirt, tied up like a noose in her navel. "I did not call the handyman." She stood in front of him, in a foreign accent that seemed to stress every word. "What do you want?" she said, like asking why he'd been born.

Don leaned forward, his response waiting for him somewhere above the bar. From a man who usually found coincidence an affliction, there were times when its beauty left him speechless. She placed the beer in front of him. "Mercy," he said.

"*Merci,*" she replied, and walked down the bar.

Seven

SCENE 27

Don watched her walk to the sunlit front, taking dirty glasses off the bar, pushing them through the sink, the light through her hands through the water. She looked up and caught his eyes and he stayed there a moment, not smiling, not saying anything there. He turned back to the bottle she'd left him, a Mohrbeer, and pulled up a stool underneath. Slowly he raised his hands forward, his arms circling the bottle, trapping it, for several seconds watching it breathe, then finally and at once he wrapped his hands to the glass, his fingers around the neck, lifting it up, drinking half.

A phone rang, the girl at the desk at the window, another desk in front of hers, computers and fax machines. Don guessed it was election time again. They had elections for everything in Crumbtown, lottery aldermen, tobacco inspectors, sanitation chancellors, elections for blackjack dealers and oyster fishermen. Every few months Maury Threetoes would set up a desk in Gloria's, with flags and pictures all over, whatever Democrats were going to win. He even had Don elected once, in 1989, for highway advocate. Don didn't know he was running until he saw his picture in the bar's window: "Don Reedy for a Smooth City." They threw a party in his new office on Washington Street. He never went back.

Don took another drink, even better than the first, washing out the morning with it. He drank again, the beer going all the way to the floor, like losing twenty pounds. That's what the dark bars were for. It didn't matter what you'd done outside. When you walked into Gloria's, you left it behind, a hero's welcome just for closing the door.

He looked around the bar, no election posters now, no names and flags to let you know, just a lot of yellow fabric on the walls, like a parachute had landed there, covering everything except the mirror behind the bottles, and the old painting in the center, that he'd seen in prison dreams, of low hills washed up on a brown beach.

He leaned forward, watching the bartender at the window, her hands on her hips, the sun through her skirt, the outline of her legs, perfect legs, he thought, except where one was longer than the other. Then he realized, the legs weren't crooked, it was her skirt, higher on the right like it had been cut that way. Funny he hadn't noticed that. All the women were probably wearing crooked skirts now, and nooses in their shirts, and speaking in thick Slavic accents.

He leaned over further, waiting for her to look up. She was waiting too, something in the window, someone she knew. The light shifted, a cloud coming through, he caught her face in the glass, a few seconds, seeing herself. He raised his empty bottle, "Hello." She didn't look over. He waved the bottle louder, "Hello."

"What do you want?" she said.

"Mohrbeer."

She dropped a glass and turned around. "I give you beer." She started toward him. "You want more?"

"Yes, I do."

Standing in front of him now, "You are following me?" she threw her towel on the floor. "Yes?"

"Okay."

"First outside, then you come in. Yes?"

He looked out the other window, the desks by the door. The painters scraping new paint off the glass. "Yes," he said.

"Why?"

"I wanted to tell you," he pointed below the bar, "your skirt."

"What?" She looked down, smoothing the sides. "What?"

"It's crooked."

"It is design," she grabbed his bottle, breaking it with the others.

"It's nice."

"You may go." She pointed at the painters. "I am not in the mood."

Don stood. "Okay." He stepped back. This bartender was not from Crumbtown, that was obvious, but she was Crumbtown. He looked out the window. He didn't want to leave. "Look, I didn't know you worked here."

"And you wear this suit," she said. "You follow me with this suit."

He pulled his jacket straight, "What?"

"You make yourself, yes?"

"Lady, this is a thousand-dollar suit."

She took a beer from the cooler and set it in front. He couldn't tell if it was for him, or her. "It is very nice," she said.

He checked himself in the mirror, behind the tequilas, his jacket so wrinkled, like the bark on a tree, open holes in the elbow, other holes patched with dirt. He appeared to have been run over by dozens of cars. His hair was soaring, cheeks pocked with stubble, a lunatic's face. "Fifteen years ago," he said, adjusting his tie, three times. He gave up and pulled it crooked, laughing at the picture, laughing like a lunatic. "I'm Don," he said, "Don Reedy."

"Really?"

"Reedy."

"The Don Reedy that is in prison."

"I got out this morning. TV parole."

"Of course," she said. "Where is your desk?"

"What?"

"Your TV show. This is your office." She gestured at the computer by the window. "That is where your director sits. You need desk. You have secretary too."

"Really?"

"Reedy. I should blame you." She walked to the register and took out his six dollars. "For what is bar without desks and phones ringing always." She filled two glasses with vodka and pushed one in front.

"What's this?"

"We have rule, you get out of prison, drink is free."

"You still do that."

"It is rule," she raised her glass. "For getting out."

He raised his. "And when do you get out?"

She picked up the empties, "I do not get out."

"What's your name?"

"Rita," she said, and turned away, walking the long bar to stand in what was left of the sun.

28

She stood at the window watching two women run past, their arms full of cardboard, chasing a bus up Lemmings. Little Angelo stumbled by, the second time today, and stopped and pressed his bent nose against the glass, waiting for Rita to forgive—she'd thrown him out twice last night. Rita shook her head and he continued on, bending after every step, for cigarettes and papers and pieces of glass. Three girls passed in front, going home from school, uniforms like Rita had to wear in Odessa, the first clothes she made herself, the singing workers' parades, the joys of steel festivals.

She glanced to the mirror beside her, to the back of the bar, the man drinking his beer, the famous Don Reedy. She'd thought he'd be older, the stories she heard, the old papers on the wall. He was tall and with a good face underneath, she could tell. Maybe men did not age so quickly in prison, only when they get out. He must have been in a long time. The way he was looking at things, her chest, her skirt.

She turned back to the window; she'd had enough problems with men who were in prison. Just look at her record. Her boyfriend Victor she had met not long after his release, six months for running a music store without a driver's license, because he couldn't pay off the police. Misha had been to prison as well, one week for cementing himself in Red Square. The magazine where she worked staged the whole thing, Misha's arrest, and the party after, their Summer of Loud issue. Misha had the loudest voice, shouting his poems like he was being stabbed. Rita's picture was there, too, she had the loudest clothes, her shirts of burning flags. The party that night when Misha wouldn't stop talking, until she kissed him under the overpass, and then every doorway on Gregor Place.

In that summer, when things happened, you did not try to stop. They were married the next week, by a priest who played in the club. The wedding lasted until October, then one morning it was done, like the magazine, like the whole country. She took a job translating American wire services for a business group. Misha sat in the room, the variety shows and every-hour news from Chechnya. When the war was ended he stopped writing altogether, refused to go out, and hardly bathed. He said she killed his poems. That was when she left him, because she thought America forgot everything, and because of the picture, in the paper, of a woman waiting for a bus in New York, wearing a dress made out of flags, like the dress Rita had made for herself and kept in a box in the closet in her mother's house.

She was working in her cousin's flower shop in Brooklyn, two years when Misha appeared at her door, swearing his love, stealing her purse. Breaking everything else. She'd been running ever since, escaping from her convicts, then escaping from herself. Once that happened it was hard to stop: Iowa, Memphis, Disneyland, and Dodgeport.

The sun was passing over, down to her feet and going fast. The phone rang. She went to answer it, then remembered the girl at the desk, Rob Landetta's office. She stood alone in the middle of the bar, debating the long walk to the window, instead sliding the vodka back in line, then rearranging the others, glancing at the mirrors between her, the face of a face of a face, and the man behind that, his beer finished, watching her.

She'd dated three men since working there. No prisoners. They were in TV, of course. It was easy. They finished their shows and left. Next year, they said. Six months since the last. Three since Misha showed up. The headaches that came every day. She went to her bag and took out the aspirin, eating two. She saw the lipstick at the bottom, holding it a second, letting go. She picked it up again, putting it on in the mirror. So what if he sees her. She grabbed two more beers out of the cooler and held them up to him.

29

Rob parked the car in front of the bar, his nose pressed against the wheel, waiting for his breathing to return. "Get a hold of yourself," he said, and slammed the door. Out front the painters were gone and the window a mess. He made a note in his head to call scenery. Inside, the new office equipment had arrived, and he checked over his new desk and computer, and the table behind the wall, which held the new fax printer and phone, and behind that, in the new chair in the corner, his new assistant, already complaining about the cigarettes.

The desk was too heavy to move so he arranged his monitor and chair as best he could, to face the window, away from the bar, away from Rita. He'd been driving around Crumbtown for an hour, one dead end after another, thinking about Rita. He needed to forget Rita.

Rob turned on the computer and pushed in his disk, and when the script came up he clicked on EDIT. In the box next to FIND WHAT, he typed RITA. In the box next to REPLACE WITH, he typed MARIE, his mother's name, any name for now, a new start. He had to finish this scene. "Okay, let's go," he said, staring at the screen. Minutes passing, wordless. Then an image developing, from his earliest memory, of his mother dancing. He must have been three or four or five, and he was sitting on the toilet, his mother dancing in front of him, singing "I'm a little teapot, short and stout . . ."

Rob's assistant rang his phone, "Mr. Landetta," she yelled, "Mr. Landetta," she had to shout like this even though she was sitting three feet away. "You're supposed to be at the hotel, to pick up Little Eddy. You're showing him locations this afternoon."

"What about Don Reedy? He arrived this morning, right, I need him there."

"He's not in his room and I can't get through to his cell. The interference is much worse today." She pushed some buttons. "It's ringing. You have to speak really loud."

Rob picked up the phone, trying to hear through the static, voices fading in, music, what sounded like a Russian talk show. "Hello?" he shouted. "Are you there?" He slammed it down. "I can't work this way." He walked out the door.

30

Don was ready this time, the phone out of his pocket and the proper button pushed before the first ring was over. "Hello," he said, a buzz of clicks on the other end, a woman's voice in the static, speaking another language. More men talking, he couldn't understand. Was it Russian? He looked to the front of the bar, the man who had been sitting at the computer, who Rita said was his director, must have just left, the secretary with him. Don should have introduced himself when he had the chance, asked for a new phone. He'd been having such a good time with this bartender, forgetting why he was here. "Rita," he said, waving her close, "do you know what they're saying?"

She pressed her ear next to his, listening, "It is the taxi radios," she said. "They are in all the phones, and the music stations when the cars are passing." She pulled her hair over her ear, laughing. "How do you say it, the dispatcher, she wants car thirty-eight to pick up a woman's cat, to take it to the barber. Hahaha. And now the driver says I always get the cat. I don't want. Give it to twenty-four. He loves the cat. He has sex with the cat." Rita laughed again. "And the driver twenty-four says yes it is a beautiful cat. Twenty-four is very funny. And now the thirty-eight says he is in love with the cat of the dispatcher." Rita shrugged, "It is always like this."

Don leaned into her, "What is the dispatcher saying?"

"It is a game. She curses him but I have seen them together, here, listen, now they are passing."

The voices faded quickly, leaving only a distant buzzing, Don and Rita still listening, waiting, the phone pressed between, who would get off first. The buzz going into his arms, the bar in his side, cutting out the air. Just to turn and they'd be kissing. He turned.

She stepped back, into the register, "Music," she announced, anchoring her skirt, "the jukebox," walking around the bar to the machine behind Don, bending down to plug it in, pushing buttons like she was playing the notes.

At the first beat Don was off the stool, saying, "That's Al Green." Four steps toward the jukebox when the voice came in, stopping him in the middle of the floor. "Turn it up, Rita. Can you do that?" He closed his eyes and flattened his palms on his head. "I haven't heard this song in so long. You know Al Green, right?"

"I just played," Rita said. She walked behind the bar and reached under the whiskeys and turned up the volume. Except for them, the room was empty.

"Yeah," Don said, "that's good. I haven't heard this song in ten years. In Creosote we aren't allowed to listen to music, except what you get on TV. But I tell you Rita: Damn I feel good. A couple of beers in a dark bar on a sunny afternoon, and a pretty bartender to talk to, and the right song comes on the jukebox. I want to dance. Hey Rita, do you want to dance with me?"

Between each line that he said, Don took a long step toward her, a sudden stop, around the bar and behind, until they stood exactly two arm's lengths apart. She didn't answer, only waited with her hands holding two ends of a towel, and that same smile she'd had on since they met, that he couldn't figure out even this close up. He took another step.

She had wanted to slow things down. A slow song, she thought, when everyone knows that the slow songs only speed things up. And of all the choices she could make, "Let's Stay Together." What was he supposed to think? He was coming toward her, around the bar, talking too fast, she couldn't understand. He was behind the bar. Customers were not supposed to be behind the bar. She was not going to dance with this man behind the bar. "Wait," she said, pointing him to the jukebox. "Over there."

Don had never liked slow dancing, but now he understood that the slower you go the better it gets. After about fifteen minutes, Rita had stopped moving; for a while he thought she'd stopped breathing. Don had danced himself down to a slight tremor in two fingers and one foot that his heart was racing to control. He'd forgotten where he was; who he was. His fingers stilled, only the foot was left, the breathing next.

She was going to kiss him. The signs were clear, shaking in her legs, thumping up her back, echoing through the chest, making one noise at the top, like a stadium cheer. Too loud to keep still. She had to move, one centimeter to the right, that's all it took, just a word in her chin and he was moving too, no way to stop, the ears kissing first, then the cheeks, their mouths in the middle.

"Wait," she pushed him off, Don stumbling into the gap. She turned around the bar, out the window, "Not here." She grabbed his hand, pulling him to the back, "Downstairs."

Eight

SCENE 31

Rob searched the hotel lobby and around the front desk, the corridor of slot machines to the elevators in the back, his production assistant hiding behind the ATMs. "I'm sorry Rob, but Little Eddy's not in his room. Nobody knows where he is."

"What was your job?" Rob asked. "You were just given one job."

"To keep an eye on Little Eddy at all times."

"So where is he?"

"This is not my specialty."

A voice called from the lobby, "Mr. Landetta," the woman behind the desk. "Are you Mr. Landetta?" Rob could only see the top of her head. "There's a Mr. Don Reedy waiting in the driveway."

Rob walked outside, Little Eddy getting into the driver's seat of a Dingo Sport, "Get in Rob," slamming the door closed. "Get in quick."

"Where's Don Reedy," Rob looked up and down the street. "Where's my car."

"I'm Don," Eddy pushed open the passenger door, "get in the car."

Rob got in, Eddy pulling at the lights and flashers, flipping the signals. He put the car in reverse, ramming the concrete fountain. "Where's forward," he cried, before dropping them into drive, the little Dingo leaping at the street, the crashing of horns, running feet, a parking attendant banging on the trunk. Rob fought with his belt, "Wait, Eddy," searching for the clip, "Wait, please."

Eddy cut right, then left, his face bleached in sweat, "Before I say anything, Robby, we got to talk," sweat in his eyes and out his chin, over the wheel pressed into his ribs, "we got to talk right now." He pointed the car at a mother and stroller, missing as if by accident.

"Stop the car, Eddy."

Two more blocks, a bus, a parking meter, a tractor-trailer, Eddy shaking the wheel the way a child would, driving in the driveway, or an actor might, with the car on a trailer being towed around the city. Rob ducked as they passed under a red light.

Eddy had promised he'd stay clean, it was in the contract, drug screenings once a week, counselors on call, the long list of rules: Eddy would stay in his room. Eddy would not use the phone. Under no condition would Eddy be allowed to drive. It had been a bad day, and now Rob was going to die, "Please Eddy."

"Call me Don. I got a problem with the new script, Rob, the bank robbery scene. I say 'This is a stickup' and then the lines right after that, to the teller, the same word that Don says over and over, to all the tellers and the managers."

"The gimme gimme gimme line."

Eddy punched the horn, "I won't do it," standing up on the gas pedal. He released the wheel: a van, a schoolbus, another red light.

"Oh my God it's out of the script that's no problem I'm taking it out it's gone. And you're slowing down now that's so good. You're stopping for the light."

"How about some music," Eddy said. He reached down and turned on the heater, banging the knobs with his hand, "I've gone a lot of research, Rob: I read all the papers; I talked to the people at my AA. I know this guy better than myself, all right, and that's just not something he's gonna say."

"You're right, and look, there's Gloria's bar up ahead, just steer into that space, now push down on the brake, the brake," the Dingo banging into the curb, bouncing up and into the new awning, dragging it twenty feet.

32

Tim and Tom stood outside the bar, taking turns at the window. "Rob's in there," Tim said. "And that's got to be Little Eddy, they're sitting at the bar." He opened the door.

Tom closed it. "Is Don in there?"

"I don't see him, anyway I don't care. It's not a life worth living if a man can't go to his local and have a beer."

"Especially if that's where he lives."

"Don't worry, brother, I brought some insurance with me."

"What's that?"

"What does it look like. It's a gun."

"It doesn't look like a gun. It's orange. When did you get this?"

"I don't want to say, because it's a gift. Here."

"Put it away, Tim. I don't want it."

"You said we needed a gun."

"It's all rusted. It'll explode." Tom pushed the gun back toward Tim's pocket; Tim fought it back to Tom's, and fighting that way, they went in the door.

33

Don kissed her down the stairs to the basement, his mouth never leaving, his hands in her hair, her neck, kissing the buttons down her shirt. Nothing else existed, no boxes, no kegs, no footsteps overhead. He'd never robbed a bank, never been to prison, never been born until this basement, half an hour before. The world was a circle, his back to hers, and in its center, the knot at the bottom of her shirt that he'd been trying to untie for nearly every moment of his adult life. It was a Russian knot, unlike any he'd seen, tied so tightly he couldn't get underneath. He tried to pull the shirt over her, slipping the sleeves down her arms, but her hands at his back were as tight as the knot. He tried to forget, he moved to her skirt, but the knot kept growing.

Then it happened, a pull and a pop and the knot came apart, like a gunshot. There was a gunshot, in the bar above. He looked at the ceiling, and back to Rita, eyes closed, waiting, she hadn't heard. He kissed her again, seeing with his hands, under the shirt now, up and up, and pop, another gunshot. "The hell," she said, turning around to tie her shirt. Running up the stairs. "Rita, wait."

He caught her at the door, the two of them peering around, a man in the middle of the bar, a short man, pointing a gun at another who was crawling on the floor, someone who crawled a lot like Tim, his half twin Tom not far away, hiding under a stool. "Where's my money?" said the man with the gun, shooting another round into the floor.

Tim crouched behind his brother. "There was no money, Eddy."

Don had never planned on this. That he'd have to wait in line if he was going to shoot the twins.

"Please Eddy," said a voice from the corner, the man who'd been in the bar before, the director, kneeling behind his computer. "Just put down the gun okay this is not in the show."

"Shut up," Eddy said. "It was in the newspapers, fifty thousand dollars was missing from the last robbery. That's them, right. They've got Don's money. How else am I supposed to play this?"

A pause followed, the men stumped by the question, all except Rita, who marched up to the man with the gun, holding her hand out like an angry schoolteacher, and told him to put it down, now.

"Hi," Eddy smiled, the entire width of his face. He reached up to shake her hand. "I'm Don."

Don was across the bar in five steps, punching the gun with his right, grabbing it down and away, then hitting Eddy with it, twice in the ear, Eddy staggering into the door, bursting out to the street. Don turned to Tim, still on the floor, another gun, hands shaking with it. Don kicked it away, under the chairs. "How you doing, Tim? What's it been, ten years?" He turned to Tom, hiding in Rita's skirt, "Come on out," the twins fighting for space beneath her legs. "I got a question to ask."

Rita reached down, grabbing the gun in Don's hand, "That is enough." Don slow to let go, like they were still dancing. She pulled harder, Don staring at her shirt, a new knot.

"No, Rita. I'm not finished." Then a gale of car horns blew in from the street, followed by a scream, tires skidding, another scream and a thump, like a bird hitting the window. Everyone turning to the front. "That is enough," she said, the gun in her hand, Tom and Tim running out the door.

34

Dyan Swaine tapped her fingers on the headrest, waiting for her driver, King, to return with a report, but all he did was stand in front of the car, staring at the man lying at his feet. She lowered the window, "Well, how is he?"

"It's Little Eddy," King said. "They're gonna send me back to prison for this."

"Yes, but how is *he*?"

"You saw. I hardly touched him. He's fine." King kicked the body on the ground, then bent down and lifted Eddy in his arms. "Except he's not waking up."

Dyan got out and closed the door. A crowd starting to gather, fishermen and postal workers, Chinese deliverymen on scooters. "All right everybody," she said, "this ain't a circus." She was still wearing her police uniform, and she pointed them up the street, "I said move it," until they were all out of the way except Rob Landetta, the man she'd come here to meet.

"Look what you did," Rob said. He poked Eddy in the rib. Eddy didn't move. "You killed him."

"We hardly touched him," said Dyan. "He ran out in front of us and we just tapped him and he fell down. Eddy, wake up."

"You killed him," Rob said, and sat on the curb and dropped his head in his hands. Dyan had taken over his script. Now she'd killed his main character.

Dyan lit a cigarette. She scratched her elbow, "I heard Buddy Dillinger's available. He'd be great for this."

Little Eddy opened his eyes, "Buddy Dillinger's a junkie."

"I told you he was fine."

"You saw," King said, "*he* ran into *me*."

Eddy jumped to his feet, apparently standing. "Where's my gun?"

35

Rita was still holding the gun as she poured the vodka, her back to Don, "I do not understand."

"Rita, I wasn't going to shoot them."

She drank the glass, gasping, then raised the gun to her lips, as if to drink that too. She pushed it across the bar. "I don't want this."

He pushed back, "I don't want it. Here, keep these too." He pulled his jacket off the stool and took out two more guns, setting them next to Eddy's. "And this one," he walked over to Tim's gun on the floor, laying it next to the others.

"You are carrying three guns?"

"I only came in with two," he said, "and one of them's not even real, and this one's all rusted, look," he spread his arms around the pistols and made them into a pile. "Just put them in a box or something, and I'll put on the music, okay."

"What is wrong with me? What am I doing?"

Don ran to the jukebox, "Music's going on right now." He dipped his face in the glass, "Uh-oh, you got Etta James."

She picked up an empty box, dropping the guns in. "I have a degree from the university. I speak three languages, and look at me, this place so much like where I was born, you cannot believe."

"I believe," Don said. "Do you have four quarters for a dollar?"

"All of you are giving me a headache, and I'm tired of this language, and you are not different."

"I am different, Rita. I just need some change."

"It takes bills," she said.

"Oh?"

"They all take bills," she yelled, his back to her now, arms wrapped over the machine. It was her bad luck, because he was not a bad person, she could tell these things, the way he held her, the way they kissed. But she was not going to bed with a man just out of prison. Well, maybe, but definitely not someone who in the one day he was out of prison had picked up three guns. She could understand one gun, and yes, she knew that wasn't the wise thing to say, but this is where she lived, and he was the first guy in a long time that she even considered kissing, and she could always tell her mother, "He had only one gun." But three guns was not a joke. Wherever you're from, whatever you've done, three guns was a bad sign.

He was standing over the jukebox like it was a car he was fixing, his knees bent into the bumper, the opening bass lines of Otis Redding, and Rita felt her knees bending too. They were her songs; she'd put them in herself, the ones that kept her alive, those nights when she felt the doors to the bar locked on the outside. So long since someone held her that close. Kissing a man again. He was only carrying two guns when he came in, and one of them wasn't even real.

When Don had talked the machine into taking his dollar, he looked over to Rita, wearing that same tilted smile again, and this time he understood what it was saying—that she was going to dance with him, but probably not speak with him, which was more than he'd ever asked of anyone. And while they danced, he'd quietly explain to her how he wasn't a killer, how he'd never killed anyone in his life, and all the events of ten years before, what happened at the last bank job, not to forget the three guns he picked up today. And maybe she'd sleep with him, and maybe she wouldn't, and that wasn't the most important thing now. He needed to go slow, the slow dance.

And no more Al Green. Al was a good start, but after one song he put too much pressure on the proceedings, everybody worried about why they're not kissing, and Marvin Gaye would only show off Don's desperation, and Etta James was too unpredictable. So he went with the Otis Redding, the godfather of loneliness, and under the opening notes of "My Lover's Prayer," he turned to the bar, her eyes with his, everything still there, walking toward her as the front door opened, a man filling half of it, "Gimme my gun," Eddy said.

Don went to the box on the bar and took out the nine-millimeter and pointed it at Eddy, who ducked behind the door. He pointed it past Eddy, at another man standing on the sidewalk, Rob, the director, more people behind him, Anthony King with his eye patch, the blond police captain, and parked across the street, sitting low in the driver's seat, what looked like Detective Hammamann, wearing a fake mustache and glasses. Don's whole crazy day waiting for him out there, ready to flood back in. He put the gun in his jacket and raised his hands over his head. "It's all right," he said, walking to the door, calling at the director, "I'm Don Reedy. Come on in."

Rob came up and shook Don's hand. "How about that. It's Don."

Eddy slapped Rob in the head, "Of course it's Don." He punched Don's arm. "Only Don could have taken my gun like that. The Don."

King came into the door and stopped. Dyan walking into his back. "Hey Don," King said. "I want my gun back."

"He got yours, too?"

"This afternoon," said King.

"Isn't this great," Rob said, "Don picked up two guns already."

Dyan shoved King to her right, "Wait in the car, Anthony," marching to the center of the room. "So this is the real Don."

He stared at Rita behind the sink, with every glass she washed she bent a little lower, scrubbing to the bottom, until all Don could see was the top of her hair, the tip of her nose.

Dyan pointed to the bartender, "Who's she?"

"That's Rita," Rob said.

"She doesn't look like Rita."

"I have to go to the bathroom," Eddy said.

"So go," she turned to Don, "I didn't introduce myself. My name's Dyan Swaine. I'm playing Rita in the show."

Don nodded, his eyes still on Rita, the one person Dyan didn't want to see. She already knew Rita, as well as she knew herself, the character had been growing inside her ever since she finished reading the script. Rita was about having fun; it was as simple as that. Always spontaneous, generous, her laughter infectious, a true friend, bisexual but she preferred the company of men, especially those who didn't care about breaking a few rules, all the things that Captain Palmer wasn't allowed to do. Every night after leaving the set, Dyan sitting alone in the hotel, the takeout Chinese and the cop channels on TV.

Rita picked up the towel, her back to him now, wiping at the register. Don followed her hands to the hair above her neck, over her ear, the scene repeating in the mirror, a little further each time. Another song from the jukebox, Delamar Harris, "How Do You Start Over When You Can't Stop." She filled her glass and swallowed it down.

"I love this song," Dyan said, her hip banging into Don's leg hard enough to make him turn, the cop on his arm, from the TV set that morning. A beautiful cop. A TV captain.

"Can I see your palm," she pulled his hand up to her eye. "I heard that criminals have an extra line. Would you look at that, it's the same as mine." For ten years she'd kept this Rita locked up, the girl she used to be, waiting tables on Avenue A. Sneaking into clubs after work, dancing all night, sleeping till three. "Hey Don do you want to dance?" She grabbed his other hand, swinging his arms, "Come on," her hips right to left.

"This is a little fast," Don said.

She moved his hands to her back, "How about this?"

Eddy locked the bathroom door, groping his pockets for the ribbon of foil, cutting it with his finger, the man in the mirror. Your name is Don Reedy, he said. You just got out of prison. The streets you used to run, now everything's different. He pulled out the keys to the Dingo and dipped in the flat side of the ignition, turning it over in the powder, up and up to the eyes in the glass. You meet this bartender, Rita. One look and you know. She sees right through. He dipped the key again, another turn, folding it in. They want you to go back, you can't go back. She's the only one who understands that, who sees what's lying in your heart, where no one's ever cared to look, so long as you got your lines right, danced for the camera. Rita knows that. She knows. You ain't never gonna do that dance again.

He burst out of the bathroom and stopped, wiping his nose until the room slowed, Don and Dyan dancing by the jukebox, Rob at his computer, Rita behind the bar. He climbed on a stool in front of her, slapping himself in the chest like he just hit a home run. "Rita, Rita," he said, then three more times again, waiting for more words to come. "What can I say?"

She filled her glass a third time, drinking it quickly, then wiping her hands on her pants. She looked over to the back corner, Don's arms wrapped around that policewoman, her hips bouncing against him like she was going up the stairs. Rita turned to Eddy. "Will you dance?" she asked.

"You mean the Dance. I don't do that anymore."

"Dancing," she said, walking around the bar, shoving his hands behind her back, the same way Don was holding Dyan. She pulled him into the middle of the room, Eddy twitching in her arms. At one point she had to stand on his feet. It was like dancing with a spring.

Don saw Little Eddy's arms around Rita's back and in response he moved his hands down Dyan's. Eddy imitated Don perfectly, holding Rita by the waist. Dyan saw that and she lowered her cheek to Don's shoulder. Eddy tried to get

Rita to do the same, his hand behind her head, pulling it down.

Rita pushed him in the chest, shoving him back. He moved toward her and she shoved him again, walking to the closet in the back corner, opening the door. She said something to Joe Far, who slept in the closet most evenings until ten, then she grabbed her sweater, putting it on in the mirror, Don and Dyan behind her, still dancing. She walked around the bar and up to Eddy near the front door, standing over him, three inches taller at least. She shook her head and walked out, Eddy running after.

Don watched her leave, then Eddy; he watched the door close, the door closed. Dyan Swaine stepped out of his arms, exhaling dramatically, "So what did you just get out of prison or something?"

He walked out the door, searching the street. They were gone. He turned into Lemmings, over the bridge, thirty blocks back to his hotel.

ACT III

Nine

SCENE 36

Rita opened one eye to see Little Eddy sitting in flowered boxers at her kitchen table. She opened another to see her husband Misha cooking at the stove, singing Willie Nelson in demented-sounding English.

"Good morning Rita," Eddy said. "Misha's making us the famous Russian eggs."

"Good morning," said Misha as he carried the pan to Eddy's plate, spooning out the red scramble. "I forgot key and your friend Don here was thanks enough to enter me the door."

"The man says he lives here so I let him in," Little Eddy said, "then he says he's your husband, and I'm like, yo, where's my pants, I gotta go. But Misha here says it's cool, how you two have this open relationship, and I wish I could get Ava going with that, but it ain't gonna happen. Not that anything happened, Rita, because you got so drunk in that Russian place we went to. I didn't think you'd make it back."

She brought her legs to the bedside, the same stockings she'd worn the night before, a new hole over the big toe. "We are separated," she said to Eddy. "I want to get a divorce but we have to go back to Russia for that." She bent over to put on her shoes, her head hurting so much she wanted to cry. "I move, and he follows. I cannot get out."

"I hear that," said Little Eddy.

Misha walked over and handed her a cup of coffee. He placed the plate of eggs by her hip. "I love you, my Rediska," he said in Russian, "and that is why I have poisoned the eggs."

"Get out," said Rita.

"What did he say?" asked Little Eddy.

"He poisoned in the eggs."

"Special Russian eggs," said Misha.

Little Eddy stood. "Where's my pants. I got to go."

"He did not poison," said Rita, "he just talks and talks like this."

"That's cool," Eddy said, grabbing a shoe, a wallet, a sock, scrambling down the stairs, hopping on one foot across the street.

Misha sat at the table, spooning the eggs to his mouth, filling it up, he said, "This Don Reedy, I don't believe he's a bank robber."

37

The morning sun bounced off the street and into the bar, where it fell upon Rob sleeping on his keyboard. A phone rang and he opened his eyes and threw himself from the table, a little voice saying, "Will you hold for Brian Halo."

"Yes, I'll hold," Rob said.

Brian Halo came on, his helicopter phone. "Rob, about these rewrites."

"I'm just finishing them, Brian Halo. I've been up all night and I was just finishing right now." Rob poked at his cheeks.

"That's okay. Dyan just sent over the changes you two worked on. Rob they're terrific."

"I didn't make any changes with Dyan. She took my disk when I refused to have Rita run over Don."

"I love that scene," said Brian Halo, "and Rita being in the gang and robbing the banks. Rita punching out the mob boss. What a character she's become, always telling everyone what to do. She's a pistol, Rob, everything I hoped for; you did it."

"I didn't do anything."

"And to think I was going to fire you this morning if I didn't get these in, and instead I've already told three people today how much I love you. Now get back to work. Dyan has sketched in what she wants; you just fill in the dialogue."

The phone clicked off and he returned his head to the keyboard. How many hours had he slept last night, how many in the last month? For what? He thought back to the excitement of that first day, hearing the story in the bar. It was in his hands then, the weight of the words, he felt the world waiting. The same way that Don must have felt holding that bag of money in the bank, about to throw it to the people. Rob opened his eyes, the pile of papers at his elbow, the script that he first titled *Crumbtown.* If anyone should be writing this with Rob, it was Don.

He stood and looked at the clock, time to go to the set, rehearsals for the first bank robbery, the biggest scene in the show and Dyan wasn't in it. He'd ask Don's advice; they could work together on the script. No, they'd work without it. Rob picked up the pages and threw them in the air, white sheets covering the tables and chairs, falling to the bar as the front door opened, a man who had to stoop to get in. It was Arnold, the owner's son, the man who'd broken Rob's foot two months before, now staring at the mess on the floor.

"What?" Rob squeezed his head under the desk, covering his face with his hands. "What do you want from me?"

"I am driver," Arnold said, walking around the computer to grab Rob's arm, "to take you to the set," pulling him to the door.

38

Don sat in his bed, the striped walls of his room, the phone again. He stood and walked to the window, the phone still ringing, Rita Bell, Rita Bell. He had to stop thinking about her, the scenes he kept running over—kissing in the bar, dancing down the stairs, the knot in her shirt, streaks of black light to the moment she walked out. Don punched at the wall, two rights and a left, his little cell.

The phone stopped ringing. Then started again. Could it be her? He traced a path in the carpet, window to bed and back again. He had to forget Rita now, forget Tim and Tom, too, forget the guns. Only one thing mattered, staying out of prison. From what Don could tell, TV was a lot like Crumbtown, only more so, easier to get lost in, the lines between the laws. One minute you think you're playing a winner, the next you're underwater, ten years in a cell trying to remember. He needed to get a hold of the script, find out what the story was, why anyone would want to make a show about Don's life. Then he'd call the mayor, Maury Threetoes. Twenty years he'd been loyal to Maury, never asked for anything. Don wanted to disappear.

There was a house upstate, a hideaway on a hill. Maury called it the Gail. He took Don there once, showed him the key, said anytime Don needed. It was Maury's way of saying he was one of the family, the lost son, the fourth toe. Maury always sent him bagels on his birthday.

The phone on the desk stopped and was replaced by a ringing in his jacket. Don pulled out his phone, pushed the button, a voice inside saying his car was downstairs, to take him to the set, car number thirty-eight. He walked to the desk, his face in the mirror, a wallet, a key, and a gun. He'd stop by the bar in the evening, the afternoon if they finished early, already planning what to say to her, how to make it right. They'd go to the Gail together, when all this was done. It had a Jacuzzi and a wine cellar, Maury had been talking about putting in a pool. Don picked up his wallet and shoved it in his pocket. Just be yourself, he said, and picked up the gun, putting it inside his jacket.

39

Tim grabbed Tom under the arms to hurry him along, past the large trailer marked "Don," and the larger trailer next to it, which looked more like a horse carrier and was divided along the side by six thin doors, each with a name taped on the front: Bank Manager, Security Guard, Teller One, Teller Two, Happy Jones, and on the last door, two names, Renaldo and Cam.

"You see that," said Tim.

"Happy gets his own room, the prick."

The twins each wore fluorescent orange vests tied over their jackets, the word "Parking" printed on their stomachs.

"Well we're supposed to drive them to the set then let's do it," said Tom.

The trailer door opened, and the actor playing Renaldo

stepped onto the top metal step, turning to yell at the man inside, "Stop crying. I can't listen to it anymore. I'm going now."

Tim stretched up his hand, "Hi, how you doing?" Tom did the same. "We're the original bank robbers of the story, the guys you two are supposed to be playing."

"Thanks, I don't need any parking."

"We've also been hired as consultants," said Tim, "to help the characters with any details."

"You could help me, " Renaldo said, "five years, a dozen television shows and seven films, and never have I had to work under conditions like this."

"Who is it?" the voice called out from inside the trailer, the actor playing Cam. "I want to see."

Somehow they all got in, the three around the man on the bed, who stopped crying briefly when introduced to Tom. "You're the bank robber," Cam said, "Tom, right, the one that I'm supposed to be playing. There were so many things I wanted to ask."

"I'm here," said Tom, reaching out his hand.

Cam grabbed it and pulled Tom close, their balding heads meeting above the bed. Except for Tom's cervical collar, Cam's darker skin, the two could have been twins. Cam glanced at the actor named Renaldo, then out the door, turning loudly to Tom's ear, "They're trying to kill me, Tom."

"We just received the new script," Renaldo said. "He's going to be shot in the first robbery. Dyan Swaine is taking his place."

"Dyan Swaine," said Tim. "Oh boy."

Renaldo nodded, "It will be a privilege to work with her."

"I'm a dead man," cried Cam.

"No," said Tom, "it was Happy who got shot."

Cam sat up in the bed, "I'm three months behind in the rent. The guild is gonna cut off my insurance." He grabbed at Tom's vest, "If they shoot me I'm going to kill myself."

"Nobody's gonna shoot you," Tom pulled him to the door. "We're going over there right now, and I swear to God nobody's gonna shoot you."

40

The car dropped Don on Delinquency, the streets around the bank blocked off with orange cones and empty coffee cups. He walked down the trailers lined up on Lemmings: wardrobe, makeup and props, boxes of fake pistols on the sidewalk, a rack of ski masks on clothespins, drying in the wind. On the far corner he found Rob Landetta leaning on one of the trucks, waving at Don as he yelled in his phone, "I want a big explosion, Sammy, but not so big you can't see the vault door come off. Big smoke afterward . . . hold on, Sammy, I got the real guy right here, I'll ask him. Hey Don, what did you use to blow up the bank vault door?"

"We never blew up a door."

"I think you did, though. It was in the papers, wasn't it?"

Don shrugged.

"Well how did you open it?"

"We asked."

"You asked, that's right; you ask, they say no, and you blow it up." Rob turned to the phone, "Sammy, I'll call you back," and closed it in his pocket. "Come on, Don. Follow me." He started across the street, the parked trucks surrounding the bank. "They're trying to take the show from me, Don. They're taking it away from you too. It's your story. We're not going to let them have it."

"Okay," Don said. "Maybe I should read the script."

"It's too late, Don. They've already got it." Rob turned and walked ahead, up the front steps clogged with pieces of lumber and plaster statues, workers carrying up smoke machines, trays of explosives. He stopped on the top, watching Don come up. "All I care about is this robbery we're rehearsing today, that we start shooting tomorrow morning. I've given in on everything else, not this. If we get it right the rest of the show is going to write itself. I'm sure of it. We're taking it back, Don, starting now."

"I just want to stay out of prison," said Don.

"Of course you do. Just tell me how it really happened. That's all I'm asking. Come on." Rob pulled him through the open doors, the workers inside scraping windows and painting murals. Rob pointed at the lobby, "I'm using three cameras here here here and special effects people from Apocalypse Vision. The actual explosion will be after we shoot everything else just to be safe but we'll need the smoke and fire starting tomorrow, and we've got fans set up so that when Eddy throws the money the bills kind of hang there and float down slow. We did a bunch of tests; it has to be just right. That's why we're using real money, fifties and hundreds. Fifty thousand dollars' worth. Because we tried the fake and it didn't look the same. You just can't fake real money."

A young man wearing a headset and suspenders came running up and into Rob, a pile of papers falling out, "Mr. Landetta, this just came in."

Rob picked up the pages, Dyan's changes in pink and blue. "Call everybody together," he said. "I have an announcement to make." When the cast and crew had forced themselves into half a circle, Rob waved the new script over his head. "I guess everyone has seen this, and now I want you to forget it, just put it out of your mind, okay, because we are going to write our own script today. I want you to say hi to Don Reedy; he's the man who robbed this bank back in '86, and who this show is about. Let's give him a big hand." As the clapping finished, he said, "Don is here as a consultant. I want everyone to listen to him. How many banks did you rob, Don?"

"Six," Don said, "counting this one twice."

"Okay, I think he knows what he's talking about, don't you. Now Don, I want you to tell the cast where they should stand, and then give us a little run-through, just like it happened."

Don circled the lobby slowly, "The security guard stands here," he said, "and the bank customers over here." A group of about twenty extras ran in, Don forming them into a line. "All right, the bank manager goes there. Tellers over there, and that's about it."

"Looks great," said Rob. "Now where's the gang? Where's the rest of the goddamn gang?"

"They're on their way," said the boy in the headset, "two minutes."

Then the only sounds were of Don's shoes on the polished floor, everyone in the bank watching as he walked into the rays of light standing slanted by the front door. Remembering. "It's all about timing," he said. "Everything has to happen at once. One guy covers the guard. One for the bank manager, one for the door, and the one who goes straight through to the tellers."

"Where's Eddy?" said Rob. "He has to see this."

Two production assistants went to the bathroom in the back of the bank, banging on the door until Eddy ran out, stopping in the middle of the floor, "Where am I?"

"Just watch this, Eddy, please, everybody, let's be quiet," Rob pointed to the doors, "Don I want you to come in just like you did back then. This is a stickup. Wait, you need a gun, hey Sammy," Rob yelled, "bring us a gun."

"He's got my gun," Eddy said.

"That's right," Rob laughed, "he's probably got a bunch of them, hey Don how many guns did you pick up today."

Don pulled out the gun from his jacket. Everyone laughing.

"Okay Don let's do it."

He walked out the doors and crossed the street and stopped and waited one minute, to give everyone a chance to relax a little. He stared at the glass entrance, the surrounding granite, windows covered with rusted fencing—the bank in front of him, a gun in his hand, the only time in his life he ever felt in charge. He started back, his heart starting to beat, the blood marching to his head, louder with every step.

He hit the doors with his shoulder, the crack of glass breaking behind, and headed straight for the tellers, in one motion his hand in and out of his pocket, the gun so much larger than before, the barrel as wide as his arm, rising up from his shoulder, spreading apart the customers, the tellers seeing it, and hearing at the same time, three quick shots at the ceiling, cast and crew diving to the floor, Don's voice echoing in the space where they'd been standing, "All right this is a stickup."

Everyone agreed to be silent.

"Sorry about that," Don said.

Little Eddy started clapping, more applause as the cast and crew climbed back on their feet. The young man in suspenders shook Don's hand and shouted, "Mr. Reedy, your story has been such an inspiration." Others followed, including Teller Two, who'd fainted briefly.

Rob was still applauding when the twins walked in, "Hey Mr. Director," Tom said, dragging the actor Cam in by the shoulder. "What's the idea of killing my character."

"Come on, you're late," Rob pulled them toward the bank manager's desk. "We're showing these people how to rob a bank. Your partner Don has already stolen the first scene."

"Which Don?" asked Tim.

"Hey Don," Rob shouted.

Don weaved his way through the tellers around the vault, the gun raised in his hand, finding Tim and Tom at the front door.

They jumped to the side, behind an actor playing the security guard. "Don, don't," they said.

Don put the gun in his jacket and walked up and placed his hands on their shoulders, a pat, then a squeeze, the same way he always greeted them, back when they were friends, only it was friendlier then. "Ow," said Tim.

Don squeezed harder, bending them over, "I don't want any trouble," he whispered. "We're doing the first robbery now, so this is before you ran on me and you got Happy killed. We'll talk about that later. Not here."

"You swear," said Tom, "no trouble?"

"Smile for the director."

Rob stepped in, "This is great. This is why we're here. What's next?"

41

The actor playing the bank manager backed to the wall behind his desk and held his briefcase over his chest. Tom faked a punch to the man's stomach, then tickled him under the chin. "Mr. Landetta," the bank manager said, "I don't think I like working without a script."

Tom pointed to the man's ear, "Basically, I just hit him right here, and after that he does exactly as I say."

"Tom knows how to make them bleed without knocking them unconscious," said Tim.

"Mr. Landetta," the bank manager cried.

"Okay. Okay," said Rob to the men. "I understand you have to threaten the bank manager, but do you have to hit him over the head. I'm just afraid of sending too many conflicting signals here. You only hurt the bad guys, right?"

"But the bank manager is a bad guy," said Tom. "That's why I had to cut him like that, so he would look like a good guy."

Rob smiled, "What?"

Don said, "What he means is that the bank manager was in on it. He helped set the robbery up. He asked us to hit him so that the feds wouldn't suspect."

Rob turned to the crew, "Okay everyone, take fifteen minutes." He sat down in the bank manager's seat and told Don and the twins to pull up chairs. Little Eddy stood behind them, folding his arms like Don. "Please explain," Rob said.

"We robbed the banks for Maury Threetoes," said Don. "He had some outstanding loans there, and this was his way of paying it off."

"You worked for Maury Threetoes?"

"Everybody worked for him. In the banks, too. They'd report that they lost fifty grand when all we took was some files Maury needed, that the manager left in the vault for us."

"But what about the money. You threw the money."

"I threw the marked bills, mostly, that they keep in the drawers for the bank robbers. You throw a little and everybody goes nuts and no one even sees us walk out. Then it was like something we did, and once you get a good story going, everybody goes with it, especially the feds. Nobody ever saw this for what it was."

"I see," Rob pushed back his chair, hands on the table. "It was like a show."

"That's right."

"Okay," Rob said, lifting his chair, putting it down. "Okay," he picked up his script, "excuse me."

They sat around the desk, Tim, Tom, Don, and Eddy, watching Rob walk out the door. For several seconds no one spoke, until Little Eddy climbed on a chair, pointing at Don. "I knew it. When I first met this guy I said this don't seem like someone who'd be throwing his good money away."

Tim reached across the desk, faking a punch to Don's chin, "Just like old times, hey buddy."

Tom pulled him back to his chair. "You said no trouble, Don."

"That's right, no trouble," said Tim. "Anyway it wasn't our fault."

Don stared at his old friends, sitting together and talking like it was all a misunderstanding. The story had changed while he was in prison. No one had bothered to tell him. It happened so long ago. Who could remember?

He stood slowly, the gun rising from his pocket, "You ran on me," he said, the gun coming down, knocking Tim off the chair. He raised it again, this time on Tom's head, twice more until Tom was on the floor.

"Here we go," Eddy said, hopping on his chair. "About time."

Don bent over, swinging the gun under the desk, his arms striking the legs, standing up straight to kick at the twins instead, his toes hitting the floor, shins against the drawers. "It wasn't our fault," they shouted up, the same words coming out, until Don finally heard. "It was Maury who did it. Maury Maury, he set you up."

"I don't believe you."

"They're lying," Eddy said. "Let me hit 'em."

Don kicked at the twins twice more, banging his ankle on the fake wood, his heart not in it, out of breath. He sat on the chair, the gun in front of him. They weren't lying. He knew that now. In a way, he had always known.

They took turns with the story, voices under the desk. How angry Maury had been with all the publicity Don was getting, the stories in the papers, everyone always asking him what Don thinks, why Maury Threetoes couldn't be more like Don Reedy. He wanted to teach Don a lesson, that this is what happens to people who like to show up their bosses. Don never learned it because of the masks they were wearing. The security guard thought Happy was Don.

Tom raised his head above the desk. "We didn't know the guard was supposed to shoot you." Tim's head appeared next to his brother's, like they were joined at the collar, "We had no choice, Don. It was you or us. Maury's Law."

He watched the twins stand and take one step back, then two, crossing the same marble floor where Happy bled out. All the nights in prison he'd spent going over that day, never once asking himself how the cops got there so fast, how none of them were his friends, all new faces, like Hammamann's.

The twins were twenty feet away now, the middle of the lobby. "That's why we told the story the way we did," Tom said, "we made you look good, Don." His brother Tim calling across the room, "Now the joke's on Uncle Maury."

Don looked up at the ceiling, the painted sky, clouds flattened against the bricks, remembering how much he loved robbing these banks, standing there with the money in his hand, throwing it in the air, watching the people, the bills coming down. Maury told him to stop playing Robin Hood, said it was a waste of escape, it wasn't respectful. Don didn't want to stop, didn't think it was that important. One of those little things that make the outside of prison different from in.

"Don," Eddy's voice standing behind him, "Don come on," moving around in front of the desk, pointing at the twins, "you're just gonna let them leave?" He followed Don's eyes to the ceiling. "What's wrong with you?" Eddy picked up the gun and shoved it into his pants, shaking his head a little as he walked away. "I got to do everything myself here."

42

Rob walked out the doors and stood on the steps and stared at the sun until his head felt significantly worse. What he thought was real had been built out of lies, and what was real, the truth behind the lies, had been made from lies as well. He thought he'd found a story that would return television to the world, make it a better mirror. Instead he'd found that the world was also a mirror, and the only thing left that was still real was the camera, the videotape, because that never lies; it shows exactly what it sees.

He paged through the script, the changes that had taken place since the day he first heard the story, the changes telling their own kind of story, of Rob's surrender, of going from director to directed, of letting himself become a player in his own show. Waiting for the camera like everybody else. Well he wasn't giving in yet. No script, no true story to back him up, but he still held the camera.

He stepped away from the doors and looked back into the bank and saw exactly how it would happen, the vault exploding, bills floating in the air, the crowd inside caught like barn animals in the hot light, men and women tearing at one another, unsure whether to stay and get the money or run from the flames. The masked men running from the old building, getting into the car as the cops pull up and give chase, the flames spreading to the second floor. He was going to need more fire.

The boy in suspenders came up and said, "Ready in five minutes." When Rob didn't respond, the boy said, "Are you all right, Mr. Landetta?"

"Where's the cop who's supposed to be watching over Don Reedy. Is he here?"

"Detective Hammamann. He's sleeping in his car the last time I looked."

"I want to talk to him right now. And get me some new bank customers, these don't look hungry enough to me. I want starving bank customers, no more actors. And where's Sammy the Robot. Let's see those smoke machines going. What are you waiting for?"

43

Don sat at the desk, the bank manager waiting for him to get up, the customers in two rows in front of him, arms hanging like a jury just back with the bad news. The same people who were cheering him five minutes before, when he shot up the bank, had just watched him beat up his friends. He looked over to the front of the lobby, Rob standing at the doors with Detective Hammamann, each of them glancing in turn in Don's direction. It was all coming down, like it always did, only faster this time. Don stood and raised his hands as the detective walked in, frisking his pockets. "Where's the gun?"

"I don't have a gun."

"Okay, I'll tell the director you don't have the gun. He wants me to stay with you from here on, says you're becoming a negative influence on the proceeding. What did you say to him?"

Don shrugged.

The detective dropped himself into the chair, big hands folding behind his head. "Remember when I arrested you,

Don, outside this bank, and all you kept saying to me was how you were going to kill those two that got away. You wouldn't tell me their names, saying you'd take care of it yourself, but where is the resolve now, Don. After what they did to you, those two standing right there." Harry pointed at the twins in the corner, shaking his head. "I tell you there is a crisis in this country."

The production assistant with the suspenders raced through the lobby, yelling at his hands, "Okay everybody, rehearsal starting, one minute."

Harry stood. "Come on, over here." All the preparations he'd made, the new suit he was planning to buy for Tim's funeral, Loretta wearing that black dress he'd seen in her closet, the day he broke into her house, lying in her bed with the clothes piled up on top.

He led Don to an open corner by the vault, holding him by the shoulder. "So since I have to take care of you myself, it means my fees will be doubled, fifty for the first day, but from now on it's one hundred." He buttoned Don's suit, brushing off the front. "I'll be honest with you, Don, up to this point you've been a big disappointment."

44

Outside the bank, Rob angrily circled the three actors, Eddy, Renaldo, and Cam, everyone waiting for the man playing Happy to show up, the rehearsal to start.

"Happy is sick," said Rob's driver, Arnold, the bar owner's son, slowly climbing the steps. "I am ready to be Happy."

"What's wrong with him?"

“He cannot act. He is very sick. He leaves now. I will be Happy.”

Sammy the Robot came by with the guns and handed one each to Renaldo and Cam. Eddy waved him off. “I’m all set,” he said, showing Sammy the nine-millimeter. “Also me,” said Arnold, who pulled out a .45 caliber.

It was just a rehearsal, but the actors in the bank couldn’t have looked more real: the tellers carefully balancing their contempt, the customers seething languidly in the imaginary heat. On the steps outside, Little Eddy finished twenty push-ups and jumped to his feet, “Let’s go,” clapping his hands, “come on come on,” slapping each robber in the back as they went through. He waited two beats and charged in, pulling the gun as he walked, as he’d seen Don do, his arm in one motion unbending forward, like he was being pulled. Don had made it look like a fight, like he was holding the gun back from firing. Eddy tried to do the same and lost badly, the gun flying out of his hand, to clatter on the floor, one bullet squirting out with a roar, across the room past the bank manager at his desk, and through Cam’s shirt and into his back.

“Oh shit,” Little Eddy said.

Rob and half the crew ran crowding into Cam standing next to the desk, Don and the detective lifting the actor’s shirt over his head, a hole like a new nostril between Cam’s ribs, blowing pink bubbles down his back.

“Do you mind if I sit,” Cam cried.

“Of course,” said Rob. He turned to the boy in suspenders. “Ambulance?” he said.

"I'm trying to get through."

Tom ran in from the corner, helping Cam into a chair. He glared at Eddy, then Rob, "You bastards," he said, "you shot me in the back."

"I want these twins out of here," Rob said, "clear the area." Arnold grabbed Tom's arm and helped him walk to the door. On the way outside, he grabbed Tim's.

Cam raised his head. "It's okay, Mr. Landetta. I think I'm okay," he said. He tried to stand and stood. "Really. I'm all right. I can do it," covering the hole with his hand.

"Are you sure, Cam. It looks like it went in your back there."

Cam took three steps and turned around, three steps more, "I'm fine. Please. I really need this job."

"What do you think, Detective?"

"I'm no doctor," Hammamann said, "but I once saw a man with the same wound doing the cha-cha at a Mexican wedding. You can never tell."

"Okay, we'll get back to work then," Rob said. "Cam, you sit this one out, you just let the paramedics take a look, is that all right with you, Lieutenant?"

Hammamann looked around the room. It wasn't all right. He was a police officer. A man had been shot. Someone had to be arrested. Harry always prided himself on knowing who could be arrested and who couldn't. He picked the gun off the floor, put it in his pocket. Then he walked over to Don and grabbed his arm. "All right come on."

"I didn't shoot him."

"You know the rules, Don. Special parole. Don't make this any harder." He was going to have to take care of Tim himself. Don wasn't up to it. Harry could see that now, Creosote had taken the man's heart. Do enough time and you never get out, a life sentence. "Come on, Don," gripping the arm tight, past Rob and Little Eddy, all eyes on the floor, to the front of the bank, Cam near the door, his head in the arms of the security guard.

"For God sake," the guard sobbed. "Why aren't we helping this man."

"Where's the ambulance?" Rob said.

"Really, I'm all right," said Cam.

Harry stopped at the top of the steps. "Just remember, Don, when you get back to prison, that they have to pay you for a whole week. Even if you only worked one day. It doesn't matter how many days, if it's less than a week, then they pay for the whole week." He searched Don's pockets, pulling out two twenties. Hc searched his own pockets, pulling out the keys. "All right. Where's my car?"

45

Once Arnold had deposited them outside the bank, Tim turned to Tom and said, "Now look what you've done." They stepped down the stairs to the bottom, where they were run into by Sammy the Robot, who asked Tom to quickly drive the detective's rental to the storage lot on Louie, where the spare ambulance was parked. Sammy said to make it double-quick since every mother on his radio was screaming for an ambulance. The twins walked to the car, Tom having to listen to Tim talk about how proud he was going to be assisting Dyan Swaine on the set, how people working on location were always having sex. Then Tim started again the story about giving Dyan cigarettes, and it became too much for Tom, who wrenched the gears into reverse and kicked the gas.

The car leapt into Lemmings, its front end swerving a moment before straightening. Tom touched the brakes briefly, then back to throttle, still gaining speed as he reversed into Dyre, the transmission howling.

"There's the ambulance," said Tim as they drove past the lot. "Stop, Tom. Didn't you hear what Sammy said? All right, that's it, stop the car."

Tom buried his chin deeper into his collar, chewing his arm as he curled onto Van Brunt, his right foot never giving up. He was one of those people who drove better in reverse, a talent that kept him regularly employed among the production companies shooting there, who were always needing cars and trucks parked and backed up.

"Stop the car, Tom."

"I'm the one who made that story work," said Tom. "I'm the one who told it, and I'm the one who sold it, and this is my thank-you, a bullet in the back." He hurdled under the red light, back onto Lemmings, the bank rearing three blocks up. When he lost his temper this way he could reverse in circles up to an hour.

"I agree that it was not right the way they did that," said Tim, "because what you did for them is very important, but by the same token not everybody can be a star, Tom, the simple laws of numbers. Now let's let me do my job here. Okay?"

Tim lunged for the steering wheel, coming away with Tom's hand, the car now driving itself, striking out for electric poles and parked vehicles, then turning its attention to the man running down the bank stairs, another one running behind. The first man entered the street, turning in front of them, three strides and the rear bumper caught his knee, kicking him to the trunk, where he remained until Tom's brother was fought off, Tom's hand once again steady on the wheel, passing the bank without slowing down. Tim pointed to the man on the trunk and said, "Now look what you've done. You've run over Don."

46

Don had been waiting with the detective for the car to be brought back, Harry holding tightly on his arm while Don went over in his head all the things that had gone wrong. From the moment he stepped out of prison he'd been a step behind everything, acting without thinking, actions that made him feel so apart, like someone was pointing a remote control, clicking RUN IN, or SHOOT, or RUN AWAY.

They watched the detective's car turn onto Lemmings, backing toward them, Hammamann starting him down the stairs. "All right, Don." And then it happened. No decision. Just a click. He was twisting his arm free, running down the steps, words shouted after, "Where are you going?"

Away through the parked cars and into the street, the wind under him, the fear making him lighter, like he was eighteen again, remembering how he used to love running from the cops. After half a block it was all behind him; he was going to find Rita, and the thought of seeing her again made him go faster; it carried him off his feet. He wasn't running anymore; he was being taken, on the trunk of a Palais Royale, wondering at how much faster things happened now than he remembered, how long his days were outside of prison.

47

"Don't stop the car," Tim said, the two men twisting their necks to see through the rear glass, Don struggling to hold on. Tim opened the window and leaned out and yelled, "Don, do you still want us dead."

Don held the antenna with both hands, his back on the window, his feet on the trunk. He looked up at the sky, the speed of the car, the wind in his eye, letters and numbers rolling over him, fingers pushing the buttons, back to prison again.

Tim slid in from the window, "I think you stunned him." He bent over the dials of the radio, "How about some music," tuning through the Russian taxis to the booming voice at the end, Detective Hammamann's voice, explaining how if his car was not returned to the bank immediately, and with Don on it, the twins would be charged with the following crimes: grand larceny of a police rental, hitting and abetting an escaped prisoner, speeding backward on a television set.

The car swerved right as Tom twisted himself further to see around Don, "All right, now what are we going to do?"

"We got no choice." Tim picked up the microphone, he pushed the button, "All right, Hammamann, we're coming in." He dropped the mike and looked at Tom. "I hate that son-of-a-bitch detective, but at least he's not trying to kill me."

48

Detective Hammamann put the radio back in his pocket, pulled out his gun, and walked down the steps into the street the way Lieutenant Gates did it on *Ten Thirteen.* He stopped and stood in the center of the road with his legs apart, raising his gun at the spot where he expected Tim would be. The scene was set, this was his test, Loretta couldn't have written it any better: Tim in a stolen cop rental, driving an escaping felon, driving right toward him. Hammamann had never shot anyone, but he couldn't hesitate now. He might just shoot Don and Tom while he was at it. The proof of his love. He wouldn't be able to go to the funeral, no Loretta on his shoulder, no picnics by the river. Months they'd have to stay apart, years, a love in secrecy, just like they had now. No greater test than that. He watched the car make its turn, sighting his gun on the passenger window.

49

Don held the antenna with both hands, his back against the trunk, staring at the power lines passing over, three per block, cutting the sky into squares, equal sections of the same picture. They turned onto Lemmings, his legs riding over the side, pulling himself straight to look down over the end, the bank five blocks away. He was going back to prison again, five years, maybe more, to lie in his cell and think about his one day out, how he managed to replay every mistake he'd ever made, like the last forty years were just a rehearsal, the sad story of Don Reedy, a life in twenty-four hours.

He just never caught up. Except for his afternoon with Rita, and crashing through the doors of the bank. These were the only times he'd felt in control. Everything else he'd been playing from behind, reacting when he should have been acting. The director was going to blow the vault, throw real money in the air, fifty thousand dollars' worth. All Don had to do was look tough and go along. They were giving him the best part, the lead, a chance to start in front, and he missed the bus, and there wouldn't be another. He lost the girl and he lost his boss, lost his parole, lost his gun. A loser's ending. Again and again.

He lifted his head from the trunk, Harry Hammamann waiting in the street, gun raised, standing like a cop. Two blocks. Don rolled to his chest, pulling himself to the roof. Not like this, he said. He'd rather be shot. And he wasn't running away. You can't run with nothing. When you're playing from behind you're just waiting to get caught, going to prison for all the wrong reasons. Because the only way to get ahead was to stay in front. Maury's Law. Take the lead and never give it up. They were using real money in the robbery scene. Tomorrow morning. If he made it that far. Don was going to take it back.

He leaned over the driver's-side window and reached in and grabbed Tom's foam-padded cervical collar, twisting it once around his fist, feeling Tom's breath catch. "Stop the car."

Tom let go of the wheel, punching at Don's hands, his face, Don twisting tighter, "Just stop the car, I'll let go if you stop the car." Tom's cheeks turned pink, then grape. He stepped on the brake, crying with the air coming in, Don's head climbing through the window, into the backseat, twisting the collar again, his other arm around Tim's neck, "It wasn't our fault," said Tim.

"It never is," Don said. "We're going to the piers."

And that's when Hammamann began to shoot, the bullets striking the bus on the corner, a fake dry cleaners store, a no parking sign. Tom shifted into drive, the car shooting forward.

Ten

SCENE 50

Rita had to walk through a thicket of metal poles to get to the front doors of the bar, men carrying in coffeemakers and lighting equipment. Inside, the front tables had been taken out with the computers and phones, and in their places stood two racks of clothes, a rainbow of rayon slacks and bowling shirts. She walked up to Joe Far, sitting at the bar, another man standing next to him, applying makeup to Joe's face. "No. No. Too much," Joe winced. He turned to Rita. "They only let me work if I'm in the show."

She hung up her jacket, about to wash the glasses when she noticed a woman standing next to her, behind the bar. Tall and young and somewhat oriental, very pretty, with a furry green shirt tied at her waist, the tattoo of a caterpillar hanging off her hip. She glanced at Rita and then went back to the mirror, adjusting the skin that was closest to her lips.

"What are you?" Rita asked.

"I'm the bartender."

"You are bartender?"

"That's what they tell me."

"Rita," yelled Joe Far. "Please you come here." He pointed to the next stool. "Please, you fired. I'm sorry. They tell me this morning. I tell them to fire me too, but they say I have to be on TV. I think it's important, don't you. My family will see, they will understand." Joe lifted Rita's hand. "I'm sorry, Rita. You're the only good person."

The makeup man returned and began spreading Joe's cheeks with glue. "Enough," said Joe. He pushed the man away. "No beard."

Rita stood and turned to go. Then stopped. Where could she go? Joe grabbed her arm. "Have a drink, Rita. Have one drink with me. Quickly. They start shooting show." He shouted over the bar, "Two vodka martinis. Do not shake."

The bartender spoke to the mirror. "What did I tell you already?"

Joe raised his fists and shrugged and turned to Rita, "She say she not really a bartender. She only plays one for TV."

51

Tom drove down Lemmings to the water, a right on Marginal, under the factory bridge, stopping at the broken gates. Don pulled tighter on Tom's collar, Keep going, he said. Down the long rubbled drive, brick walls towering on either side, hooks rusting over crumbled arches. At one time the largest maker of erasers in the world. When they were near the end Don told Tom to stop, then reached over and pulled out the key. He climbed out and walked to the water's edge, this pier that used to go on forever, Tom yelling after, "What do you want?"

They had come here every day as kids, Don running the games, stinkball and crumbtag, crooks and robbers shooting through the arches. Happy's deaths were always the most theatrical, long writhing moaning. Tom always denied he'd been hit. Tim liked to throw himself in the water, forcing his friends to save him.

When Don was a little older, he'd come here alone, the stars on the ocean, his ships on the wind. Bringing his blanket the nights his parents fought. The week he'd spent hiding in the warehouse after his father's funeral, mid-February, until Tim and Tom told Maury, who told his mother. Taking them out for a lemon slush he couldn't touch, Don kicking Tim under the table. He wanted to kill them. Five years later they were stealing cars together, worst thieves Don had ever seen. Fifteen and they were in the banks, Maury saying what a fool he was to work with the twins.

Tom was low in the driver's seat, trying to hot-wire the Royale with a penknife. The sun behind them, windowless houses on Drywell, lines of gutters twisting up the short hill to the bank, highest point in Crumbtown. Don needed information, how they were bringing the money in and when, inside the bank or out. It could be easy, with the smoke machines going, actors wearing masks, carrying fake guns, Little Eddy holding a bag of money. It could be very easy. He needed a driver.

The engine started, Tom's head rising behind the wheel, the Royale backing away as Don walked toward them, backing into the brick wall, stalling there. Don came up to the window, "The steering's locked." He opened the door, Tom still fighting with the wheel, a penknife jammed into the ignition.

Don grabbed Tom's wrist, twisting it over until the knife fell out. "Get out of the car," pulling him out. "Let me see." He checked the lock, opening the screwdriver from the knife, working it in.

"What are you doing?" Tom said. "You've got the keys."

Don turned the wheel slightly, feeling for pressure on the blade. Twenty years since he'd jacked an ignition. He had to see if he could still do it. "I'm making a withdrawal," he said. "Tomorrow morning. The Dodgeport Savings and Loan."

Tim got out of the passenger seat, walking around to stand nervously with his brother. "That bank's closed, Don, eight years."

"I'm not robbing the bank. I'm robbing the robbery. They're using real money in the show. The director just told me. Fifty thousand dollars."

"Fifty thousand."

Don lowered his head beneath the dash, a tangle of red wire. "That's right, and I need to know the schedule there, how they're doing it. Who would know this?"

"Crazy Louie," Tom said.

"He runs the coffee truck," said Tim.

Don touched the leads and the engine kicked in. He gunned it to the water, skidding half a circle to stop at the edge, the twins in front of him, waiting for a direction. They'd never gone to prison, not one day. Don had gone four times. The fortunes of Crumbtown. Whose fault was that? He pulled up slowly. "Get in the car."

"I don't know," said Tom.

"Yeah," said Tim. "I don't know."

"I'm not asking you. Let's go."

One at a time they slid in the back, carefully buckling their belts. Don drove out the gates, a right and a left, Tim leaning forward, "Robbing a robbery," he said, "is that a crime?"

52

The bar's door slammed closed, the talking stopped, and Rita turned to see Don come in, eyes searching wildly a moment before finding hers, blinking in the lights. He was going to start in about last night, she was sure of it, all the things she'd been hoping to forget. She raised her arms, she didn't know how it would go, but when he was close, she saw they were the same eyes as yesterday evening, when he'd first asked her to dance.

"Rita I have to do something right now, with Tim and Tom, and as soon as I'm done I will come back here and I thought maybe we could have another dance. And then I could buy you dinner too, just us, like a date, and the hell with everything else."

"What do you have to do?" She held herself back from touching his nose.

"We just have to make a plan for tomorrow, and I need to make sure you have those three guns I left here yesterday. That's all. You remember? The ones you put in the box."

"I remember."

"And then I think we could go get something really nice to eat, even though it might have to be takeout, since I'm wanted by the police."

"Come with me," she said, "right now. We go to this Russian place where police are not allowed. They have music. I can explain about last night."

His pocket started to ring. He took out the phone and threw it on the bar. "I don't care about last night. Nothing happened."

"Nothing happened with me," she said. "It was a mistake." She pulled on his hand.

"I can't," he said. "Tomorrow."

"Okay then." She went behind the bar and took out the box that was under a box, and carried it to the front, turning back, "Then I come with you." She walked out of the bar.

53

Tim opened the car door, waving Rita in, taking the box from her hands as she sat in the back. "Thank God you brought some drinks, Rita. Don made us stay in the car." He pulled his rusted pistol out of the box. "These aren't drinks."

Tom sat in the driver's seat, his collar turned backward. "We're going to rob the TV show, Rita."

"That's right, they stole our lives," said Tim.

"The rights to our lives," Tom said. He looked down at the orange vest he still wore, pulled it off, and threw it out the window.

Don opened the back door and sat beside her, lowering his head to her shoulder, his knees bent up near Tim's neck, his elbow almost touching her hand. "Let's go," he said.

Tom watched them in the mirror. "Is Rita in this?"

"No," said Don.

"Yes," said Rita, their legs in the middle of the car, "I am in." Then his hip pressed hers, or she thought it did, and she had to open the window, her leg into his as she did so, and with a slap his hand fell on her knee, like a soda coming out of a machine. They both faced front. He took away his hand and she pressed again, and again it fell, and that's how it was done.

"Now," Don said to Tom. "Double-quick."

They drove through the alley to Van Brunt, a left on Louie, a right on Ralph, all the way to East Crumbtown. Rita looked out the window, the buildings sailing by. Things were going too fast; she had to slow down, stop and look at what was happening, but she didn't want to stop. She wanted to go faster. It didn't matter what happened after. She felt his hand behind her neck, past her ears and into her hair, her lips taken to his. Not a kiss, exactly, not moving, just breathing, the first time.

She opened her eyes. "How can I like you this much?"

"It's in the script," he said, and kissed her again.

54

Crazy Louie let them into his apartment and gave everyone a small seat. He took Don into the back bedroom and closed the door, "Nobody knows you're here, right?" Don shook his head and Louie went to his closet and pulled out three suits, throwing them on the bed. "First of all, I can't talk to you with what you're wearing." Louie was from Brooklyn and worked wardrobe for several years before moving to catering. He picked up the navy wool and held it up to Don, "Try that." Don put on the jacket. "Better," Louie said, and told him how and when the money was coming in, how the director planned to shoot the scene. An armored car from the mayor's office was going to be there, but Louie heard they were using actors to play the guards, to save money. Don asked him if he wanted a part. Louie said he'd take ten percent to watch, and five hundred for the suit and he'd throw in the shoes.

A crowd of twenty or more was waiting in the living room, old friends and neighbors, and when Don came in everyone threw something. Uncle Billy, whom Don wasn't related to, was the first one to punch him. He said he heard Don had died and he cried so violently it took three people to pull him away. Iron Heinz danced through the door with a case of beer on his head, and Father Sunshine walked in and wrestled with his hair. Don saw Rita sitting on the couch and had almost reached her when Mrs. Lasagna cut him off, "What's my name?" she yelled, shoving a plate of pasta into his ribs, asking him three times until he told her. Sal Melanie showed up with Dave and Mary Lynn, filling him in on the last ten years, the floods and the layoffs, their record-setting bad luck, one number from winning it all. Then everyone moved to the table, Don sitting next to Rita, her knee under the red cloth, corned beef and blintzes and veal scallopine.

55

When it was over, Tim and Tom left to hide the car and get the masks Tom had kept all this time in a bowling bag in his mother's house. Crazy Louie led Don and Rita to the door, handing him the key. "You can stay upstairs in 5B, Ms. Lee's place. She's at the hospital now. Her sister went in with the kidneys and so Ms. Lee went in with the gallstones; they always go together. I'm supposed to be taking care of that fat dog of theirs."

Louie shut the door and Don put his arm around Rita and kissed her as she turned, her ear to her cheek, the side of her mouth. When their lips finally met it was like one of the guns went off. Don dropped the box and shot both hands to her back, as far as he could without leaving her face, her hands making him tighter, pushing his hips together, down his shoulders.

There were a million things to plan out, whether to rob Little Eddy in the bank or get him coming out, and Tim and Tom to worry about, and Hammamann, and having enough bullets. But he couldn't think about any of that, only the way her mouth opened to him, giving him air, like he'd been holding his breath for forty years. He broke from her lips and picked up the box and grabbed her hand and ran to the first landing, Rita taking his to lead him to the second. They took turns like that, the last flight to the top, Rita pulling on the rail like she was climbing from a pool.

He turned the key. The apartment framed in paisley. An old dog limping up, sneezing twice. Rita said hello while Don ran to the pile of records in the corner. He didn't know Duke Ellington, but the title sounded right, *Indigos.* Everything else that he could see was Tony Bennett or Jerry Vale, and they were for different girls. He took the 45 off the turntable and set the Ellington up and clicked START. By the time the needle hit he was pulling Rita to the floor. They rolled over each other, the dog licking their arms.

Rita ended up on top, her lips bumping off, "The music," she gasped, "something is wrong."

She was right. He'd made a terrible choice. Who knew Duke Ellington was insane? The notes weren't indigo, but fast and sick, like the piano player was being hit with a hammer. "Don't worry." Don said. "It gets better later." He wanted to change the record but his shirt had just come off and her shirt was coming off too. A matter of one last button, which had turned out to be different from the others, in ways he didn't understand yet. He was trying so hard to figure out this button.

"Stop it," she said, but Don was almost there. "Stop the music." She stood, bringing the last button to eye level, where he realized it wasn't a button at all but some kind of hook, and why would anyone put a hook there. He freed it, and she was gone, the empty cloth falling over his arm, her back to him at the record player, holding up the album cover. "The song is 'Solitude,'" she said. She wore a black bra that appeared relatively uncomplicated to undo. "I think the speed is too up, but I don't see switch." She crouched down in front of the machine, white legs rising up her skirt, to show the black lace frontier of his dreams, the ten years they'd taken away. "I can't breathe," he said, and ran to her, his hand driving down.

She didn't have a lot of practice going to bed with men she'd just met. The few times before were more drunkenness than desire, a left turn instead of a right. It was very different being sober, and knowing exactly where you were going, and wanting to get there and get there fast. She'd been six months without a lover. It felt like ten years. What did ten years feel like? She knew what it looked like. The way he looked at her, like she was the reason he went to prison. And then they both tried to walk but had to run, racing up the stairs, kissing him at the top. She'd never felt a mouth so hot, not even her boyfriend Victor, who talked to Jesus in his fevers. He turned the key in the door and she thought she'd never wanted someone so much, on the floor, the table, it didn't matter, pulling off his shirt, his shoes, the sooner the better.

Then the music started, and there was something terribly wrong with it, and suddenly so many things she wasn't sure about, like was he ever going to get her shirt unbuttoned, and if he did, what would he think about her breasts, which were not exactly the same size, and when was the last time she had brushed her teeth, and nothing was going to happen between them as long as that noise was playing.

Her shirt came off when she stood, and for a moment she was afraid the woman who lived there was going to come home from the hospital and have a heart attack at the door. It was no wonder that woman got sick, listening to this music. Rita crouched in front of the record player, finally finding the switch, from 45 to 33. The record gave one last cry and surrendered. There was the piano, a simple melody, the trumpet coming in, Don kissing her again. He started with the hard kisses and then got softer, which was the opposite of every guy she knew.

The notes grew further apart, and stopped. Her skirt fell off. Don was looking at something in her hair, like he was trying to remember the name of it, his eyes drifting away even while his hands were going places that would be hard to come back from. She wondered what other women he'd known, if that's what he was thinking of. It occurred to her that ten years in prison was a very long time. She pulled his hand to her waist and inhaled deeply, and said, "Condoms."

"My God," he said, like she'd just told him of her death. "Rita, it's okay. I think it's okay." He took two steps back, one forward. He found the lame right arm of the couch and sat down.

"I'm sorry. But I do not want to get pregnant, and too I do not know—"

"I've been in prison," Don said. "That's what you mean." He pulled out a cigarette and tried to light the filter.

"No. I had a boyfriend in Russia. He was sick."

"Okay. Okay," stepping toward her as if to kiss her, she wanted him to kiss her. He picked up his shirt. "I'll get condoms."

"Stay here," she said, too low for him to know. She was going to say it louder, but by then he was out the window, climbing down the fire escape. She turned up the music, and sat on the floor, and covered her chest with her arms, thinking it was the saddest song she'd ever heard.

56

Don ran down through the jagged twilight of East Crumbtown, through the long shadows of empty stores and shuttered stores and stores that had never been open. He ran with his head in his chin, like an escaped convict, jumping around the puddles of streetlight until he got to Lemmings and stopped, looking up and down for cops. He turned south, past the glue-eyed teens circling the corner, the old men hunkered in front of stalled buses. It was a dangerous place for him to walk, but the stores were open here, and two blocks up a Sunhome Drugs sign fizzled. He broke into another run and found the doors locked, the windows empty, boxes of broken ceiling tiles, stacks of old pictures and dusty canvas, a TV pharmacy.

He turned into a side street, running out of breath, about half a block, into a little store for some cigarettes. The Chinese guy behind the counter was watching TV, and there, hanging over his head, racks and racks of prophylactics. Don ran to the cooler and pulled out a six-pack and put it on the counter with the cigarettes, and while the man counted it up Don said, "Oh yeah, and some condoms too."

"What kind you want?"

"You know, the usual kind."

"You want lubrication?"

"Yes."

"You want flavor?"

"Flavor?"

"Cherry, mint, assorted?"

"No flavor."

"Okay. You want pleasure or no pleasure?"

"Pleasure."

"Pleasure for him, or for her?"

"Can I get pleasure for both?"

"No."

Don thought for a minute. "Okay. For her."

The man put a purple box across the counter. Don picked it up and read the instructions, an uncertain deflation setting in. In his limited experience with condoms, Don had come to believe they didn't work for him, or Don didn't work for them. Every time he put one on it was like a death in the family. He took a beer out of the bag and twisted the cap. He looked over at the man behind the counter. "You want a beer?"

"Okay," the man said.

Don opened the cigarettes and offered one. They smoked. He opened the box of condoms and offered one to the man, who laughed a long time. "You very funny. I am married man. Very funny."

"I never liked these things myself," Don said.

"No problem," the old man disappeared under the counter and pulled up a briefcase stuffed with cheaply jeweled daggers and tiny brown boxes covered with Chinese letters. He pushed one of the boxes into Don's hand. "For you, for the *pinga*," curling and uncurling his finger for dramatic effect. "All night. Never fail."

Don pulled out the oval vial. "I'm supposed to pour this?"

"You very funny. No, you drink. Always effective."

He opened the stop, the smell of heavy industry, downing it with the last of his beer.

"Now go. Quickly."

Don waved to him from outside the window. Only then did he realize it was the same store he'd been in the day before, that he'd run into when he was running from the cops, the police captain tied up in the back, the man with the turban who'd pulled out the assault rifle. A TV store in the day, a condom store at night.

57

Rita was sitting on the steps of the building across the street, and when she saw Don turn the far corner, she leaned her shoulders further into the shadows, wiping her eyes with her sweater. She pushed her cheek under the railing as he passed, watching his long strides, a grocery bag bouncing off his knee. He never glanced over to where she was sitting, and even if he had, she knew he wouldn't have seen her, because she was supposed to be upstairs, waiting for him, and his eyes were already in the building, climbing, and she didn't know why she left, only that she wanted to go back, and still she stayed there on the steps, watching the door close behind him.

She had been sitting on the floor, looking around the sick lady's room, just listening to the music, waiting for him to come back, when suddenly she started to cry, and then she couldn't stop, the tears coming out of her like pieces of metal. She hadn't cried in a long time, not since she first came to Brooklyn two years before, not through all her troubles with Misha, and the sadness of the cities, the loneliness she'd found there. If Don saw her like this he'd want to know why she was crying, and she didn't know why, and she tried everything to make it go away. Then she was putting on her skirt. She was walking out the door.

She saw the light go on on the top floor, his shirt passing through. Then another light, a different room—Where is she? She saw him come back to the window, his face pressed in the glass, one eye, then the other. The light went off, one, two, three. How could she leave? She grabbed her hair and pulled it down her face. He might get arrested tomorrow; tonight might be all they'd have, and it was happening so fast, and tomorrow would only be faster, and the thought of that made her start crying again, that damn song. She had to go; it was getting cold, the wind picking it up off the water, cold steps through her skirt. She'd left her sweater up there, and where was she going. He was the first man she'd met in years, the way he looked at things, like he was giving them new names, the way he looked at her. She wanted to lie next to him, to feel him moving inside, his heart banging against her.

The door at the top of the stairs was open. She pushed in and turned on the light. He wasn't there. She picked up her sweater and put it on, walking into the little hall where she found his shoes. She followed them to his pants to his shirt, to the other room where he lay facedown in the bed. She leaned over, watching him sleep, and with her finger she began to trace his body on the sheets, starting with his foot, the outline of his leg, his hip to his chest, his shoulder, the long scar running up to his neck. She touched him there, shivery where the skin had been opened, and he groaned and she felt him shake.

She pulled the blanket up over him and he groaned again, rolled to his back, and started to snore, the blanket going up and down over his chest, and going up further down, below his stomach, rising over that space between his legs, up and up until the blanket was higher than his chest, higher than the top of her skirt, and she pushed down on it and it came right back. She walked to the door and turned around to look at him once more, before going into the other room and turning off the light and folding herself into the old couch.

ACT IV

Eleven

SCENE 58

Dyan Swaine sat in her trailer and looked for the last time upon Captain Palmer, her final day on the set of *Ten Thirteen.* She adjusted her bulletproof vest, carefully wiped clean her collar pins, then straightened the gold bars; fixed her hat. The knocking on the door increased, the girl calling her name, trying the latch, Gary joining in, the third AD, banging hard now, "Let's go, Dyan, today please." The son of a bitch couldn't give her two minutes.

She opened the door, five of them out there, not one would look her in the eye. "Where's King?"

"He called in sick," Gary said. "We'll escort you today."

She came down a step and held out her hand. No takers. "Bunch of hyenas," she said, "you can taste it."

"It's just a job, Dyan."

"Yeah, yeah, I know, let's go."

Everyone had come to see her final performance, the entire cast and crew, at least a hundred people lining the two-block walk from her trailer to the set. A few waved; Dyan tried to remember which ones. Most of the others just stood there grinning like weeds in the sun. And then someone yelled "Bitch," and another "Die bitch," and it was all over, up and down the line, Gary lamely holding up his hands, "Now now you people." She kept her head high and straight; she did not cry.

Earlier, in her trailer, she almost gave in, almost called the producer and said she'd take a cut in pay if they let Captain Palmer live. *The Real Adventures of Robin and Rita* had no script, no proven actors. She'd been worrying about it all morning. Now she was calm, ready; these people were making it easy.

59

A sporty new Dahlia stopped in front of the Dodgeport savings bank. Four actors got out and walked up the steps toward the cameras filming them from the top. The men wore black ski masks with a backward C stitched to the front, from forehead to chin. They climbed the stairs in single file: Little Eddy in front, followed by Arnold Pascovic, Renaldo Stein, and Anthony King in the back. King had been called in the afternoon before, an emergency opening for a bald bank robber, starting immediately. He often took bit parts with TV shows, his acting résumé was on file with the mayor's department of television. It listed his previous experience as a pimp, informer, and convict, and the small roles he'd played, cops and court officers, mostly. His biggest part to date, a rookie police officer shot in the chest.

At the top of the steps Little Eddy raised his hand and waited for the other robbers to line up behind. He dropped his hand, the men pulling out their guns as they walked past. Eddy followed them in.

"Cut, cut, cut," said Rob Landetta, stepping out from behind the camera, "we got them going in, and since we're here and the light's good, let's shoot them coming out. This will be after the robbery now, the vault's exploded. I need Sammy inside with the smoke machines; the flames we talked about."

The bank robbers came out and Rob leapt forward to shake their hands. "You guys were great. King, you'll be leading the way out. Eddy, you're last, maybe twenty feet behind, and you're holding the bag of money, right. Where's my bag of money, folks?" Rob walked down the steps to the car, "Okay the first three robbers come down like this and pile in the car. Eddy you jump onto the trunk and turn around to face the customers coming out. Then you take some money out of the bag and throw it in the air with a big old whoop. You toss the bag through the sunroof and dive in after. Any questions."

Little Eddy stepped forward and said, "Yeah, Don doesn't whoop."

"Okay Eddy, that's fine, whatever you think he should do."

"And Don doesn't bring anybody flowers. That's right out."

"What flowers, we said nothing about flowers."

"I'm just telling you."

Rob's assistant grabbed his arm, "The money, sir. It's over there," pointing to the armored car that had appeared on the corner.

Brian Halo sat in the back of the armored car with another man Rob had never met before, who looked and dressed like a very old chauffeur. "Rob, hi, I want you to meet the mayor. Your Honor, this is Rob Landetta. Mayor Maury has been kind enough to loan us this money, and I don't know if you're aware of this, Rob, but the mayor is the chief financial backer of this show. Without his support, none of this would be possible."

"Thank you," Rob said.

The old mayor nodded cheerfully, cheeks blown outward like he was playing a trumpet. Brian Halo opened a black leather satchel and showed Rob the bills inside, "Fifty thousand dollars, no interest, and for these favors he's done for us, the mayor has a small request."

"Go ahead."

"A very small change," said Brian Halo. "One name for another. What the mayor is asking is that everywhere the name Don appears in the script, it be replaced with the name Maury, and, of course, then replace all the Maurys with Dons."

"Can't be done," Rob said, "the bar scene we shot last night. They call him Don."

"Not a problem, we'll dub over it. Okay?"

Rob looked over at the grinning mayor. "No, it's not okay," he said, and stepped out of the doors and looked back, and with an almost audible crash the mayor's cheeks collapsed. It became, Rob could safely say, the saddest face he'd ever seen. Rob looked down at the man's shoes, black boxes shaped like the cabs of pickups.

"That's it then," Halo said. He closed the bag and bowed his head. "Show's over."

The boy with suspenders ran up, "We're ready, Mr. Landetta. The fires are going. We only have a few minutes." Rob stood at the back doors. He'd never seen the inside of an armored car before, but he doubted leather bench seats and mood lighting were standard.

"Okay," Rob said, "I'll make the change."

The mayor stood and opened his arms and beckoned Rob in. He was happy again, so much so it hurt Rob to see it, the patched eyebrows leaping up his head, cheeks blown up to painful limits. Rob grabbed the bag out of Halo's hand and started toward the set, a few steps and a familiar hand around his neck, "He's a brilliant man," Brian Halo said, "once you get to know him. The FBI has three separate investigations going against the mayor. They bugged his house, his office, but he hasn't said a word in years."

Rob looked down the street at the bank, the first traces of smoke from the front doors. "I've got to get to work."

"Yes yes, to work, and we'll use some of this footage for *The Brian Halo Show* tonight. Take some extra shots of me on the set, too, talking with Little Eddy, that sort of thing, get the publicity wheels turning. Nothing can stop us now."

60

The four of them waited in the black Cantor that Don had stolen that morning, Tim and Tom in the front, their old masks from ten years before, white skin pushing through where the moths had been at them. Don and Rita sat in the back, on opposite ends of the seat, wearing the new masks Crazy Louie had made for them, same backward C stretching from forehead to chin, Ɔ for Crumbtown. Tom smoked behind the wheel, checking the rearview mirror every few seconds, two blocks away the camera crews setting up across from the bank.

"It looks like they're almost ready," Don said. "Are we ready?"

Tim pulled his mask halfway up. "Can I make a phone call?"

"No."

"I just want to call Loretta, tell her I won't make it home for dinner."

"You haven't been home in months," Tom said.

"That's what I'm saying, they must be worried by now and I think they deserve to know why I'm late. That I'm going to be killed here today."

"Nobody's getting killed," Don said, but Tim was already running up the street, the pay phone on the corner, pushing the buttons.

"I want to make a call too," said Tom.

"Get out then," Don said. "Better you leave me now than when we get to the bank, like you did the last time." He looked over to Rita sitting next to him, face pressed against the window. "That goes for everyone who's run out on me." He waited for her to speak, her eyes locked across the street, another language.

Don had woken at six that morning and found her sleeping on the couch, shoes on like she'd been out. He took off to steal the Cantor, and when he came back she was downstairs with the twins, watching TV. She wasn't talking. He wasn't asking. Then Crazy Louie called and they were going out the door and he turned to her, You coming or not? She nodded her head and here she was, sitting next to him.

"Because I'll do it myself," Don said. "Now that I know how easy this is going to be, what Crazy Louie just said on the phone."

Tom lit another cigarette, pointing it at the bank. "What about the armored car?"

"Like I told you, actors. Hammamann's out looking for me. The guns are fake. They're being very careful after yesterday. All you do is back the car up as Eddy's coming down the stairs. I get out and take the bag. You drive us away."

They turned to see Tim walking toward them, hands in his pockets, kicking stones in front of him like a schoolboy just suspended. He sat down in the front seat of the Cantor. "Let's go," he said.

"What did she say?"

"She changed the locks and she's changing the phone and changing her name." Tim pulled the mask down his chin, buckling his seat belt. "I still don't know what she's so angry about."

61

"I'm a Don. I'm not a Maury," said Little Eddy.

"It's just a name," Rob said. "It doesn't matter." The two stood near the front doors of the bank, a thickening puddle of smoke that had taken the floor away with their shoes to their ankles.

"I'm just supposed to blink my eyes and be a Maury."

"Look Eddy, your name's not called in this scene. You can be Don here. No one will know."

"I'll know," Little Eddy began to pace, swinging the bag on vanishing legs, the smoke rolling in like breakers from the machines pumping it out near the vault, taking away the bank manager's desk, the tellers' stations, turning the bank customers into apparitions. "Oh shit I forgot my lines," Eddy said. "What are my fucking lines."

"Eddy you don't have any lines." Rob looked down; the smoke had taken his hands. In the lobby the bank customers disappeared and appeared and then were gone. From the space where they waited came angry groans, a man shouting "Where's my money?"

The boy in suspenders tapped his arm, "Mr. Landetta," all Rob could see were eyeglasses and hair. "The bank customers are becoming unruly, sir. They say they want their money now. We hired them off the street like you asked. I think some of them have been drinking."

"Okay, we're rolling, let's go." Rob opened the doors, smoke rushing for the exit, billowing over them. "Action," he shouted, pushing the bank robbers outside, down the steps, the first three falling into the parked Dahlia, Eddy climbing onto the trunk.

Rob called to the bank customers in the lobby, "Go, go," herding them out the door, the men stumbling down the stairs, stopping in a pile at the feet of Little Eddy, stepping forward as they pulled one another back. Eddy reached into his bag and pulled out some bills and held them over his head, over the men, waiting. Several moments passed. He'd forgotten what to do next. "Come on," one of them said, "gimme gimme gimme," and soon all the customers were shouting it, twisting and bowing like courting pigeons, swinging their arms up and down, the Gimme Shuffle. Eddy leaned back as if to throw the money, then clutched everything to his chest.

Brian Halo stood behind the camera crew across the street. "Keep shooting," he whispered. He watched the events through his handheld monitor, which received transmissions from the cameras, the little TV inches from his face. "Beautiful," he said.

62

"Get ready," said Don, "they're coming down the stairs. Okay there's Eddy and he's carrying the bag, let's go."

Tom squeezed the Cantor into reverse and opened the gas. Tim grabbed the dash, "I hate this part."

Don sat against the back door, his hand on the handle. He turned to Rita, the other side of the seat, still looking out the window. Not one word to him all morning.

She felt his eyes breaking in, poking around for an answer. When all morning she'd been trying to say it, waiting for the right time; now there was no time. "I am sorry about last night," she said, turning to see.

He moved closer, the middle of the seat.

"I could not stay in the room. I went outside, across the street. I watch you come from the store and upstairs in the window I saw and I waited too long. You were sleeping and I did not wake, only watching." She closed her eyes, her hand somehow knowing where to go, and there he was, all this time, his lips pressing hers through the mask, endlessly forgetting, everything kissing.

"I can't see," Tom yelled. "Get down. Get out of my way," slapping Don in the head. "I can't see." He hit the brakes, but by then it was too late.

63

Little Eddy jumped up and down on the Dahlia, a handful of money over his head, yelling to the crowd of men, "I can't hear you," their voices rising back, one indigent roar, "Gimmegimmegimme." Eddy leading them on, jumping higher with every cry. He was still in the air when the Cantor skidded into the Dahlia, the crash pushing it back just enough so that when Eddy landed it was on the Cantor's trunk. He fell against the rear window, staring through the glass, another gang wearing black masks. He rolled to his knees, gripping the bag as the mob of bank customers moved in.

Don and Rita were parted by the impact and sent to their seats, the crack of Eddy's head on the window. The door jammed, Don kicking it as he watched Eddy roll off the trunk, still holding the bag as he ran up the street, twenty bank customers chasing after. Don recognized some of them from his time in Creosote, others he knew from other times, other prisons. "Drive, Tom, what are you waiting for."

Tom pressed on the gas, the Cantor refusing to move, his foot to the floor, wheels spinning below. He shifted into low, and slowly the larger Cantor began to go, dragging the Dahlia behind them, trunks locked from the crash. Down Lemmings the short hill to the water, getting faster, passing the bank customers that were surrendering early, until they were gaining on Little Eddy.

Don raised himself out the window, the roof to the hood to the front bumper, Eddy twenty feet ahead, ten. He reached forward for the bag, almost there when he felt the car hesitate, suddenly slowing again, like they were pulling a much larger weight. It was the bank customers, all twenty of them, climbing onto the Dahlia as it passed them, clustering on the roof and doors like circus clowns.

Don crawled to the back, kicking the men on the trunks, "Get off," watching them fall only to run up again, helped back on by their friends. "Look out," said one, pointing to the street behind, "here come the cops." Everyone turning to the armored car approaching, a cameraman on the roof.

64

Rob sat next to Brian Halo on the leather bench, Maury the mayor in the captain's chair across. "What the hell happened," Rob said. "Who's in that car? Where's Eddy going?"

Brian Halo stared into his handheld television, the footage from the cameraman above. "Fantastic shot, but we're too close." He banged on the front wall of the cab, "Slow down, we don't want to overtake them."

"What are you talking about? We need to stop Little Eddy and take him back to the bank."

Brian Halo pulled Rob into the TV, "We have to use this." He banged on the roof, yelling "Closer on Eddy, that's it. Look how steady that shot is, from a camera on the roof, amazing." Halo turned to the mayor and said, "Your Honor, for an armored car it's a very smooth ride."

The mayor smiled as if he'd just been handed a small child.

"You're getting your money's worth today, Mr. Mayor. It would have cost us thousands to set this up ourselves."

The mayor's eyes doubled in size, his mouth rounding in joyful surprise. He nodded, holding out his arms for the little TV.

"Take a look."

The mayor made a face that said thank you, and then another face to show how impressed he was with the quality of the image, so clear it was almost like being on the roof himself. He watched the close-up of the little man running ahead, the view widening to show the dark Cantor in pursuit, then widening more, Marginal Street all the way to the eraser factory bridge, two blocks up. How many times had he promised to tear that bridge down? It was too low; buses had to go around, trucks getting stuck, his armored car could barely clear, he knew, less than a foot to spare. And the cameraman on the roof. They were getting closer, half a block away, the picture shrinking from the bridge, back to the Cantor. The cameraman didn't see the bridge. They were going too fast. The cameraman was going to hit the bridge.

The mayor stood and pointed up, then back to the little TV. He banged on the window that separated them from the front, pointing to the roof again.

"What is it, Your Honor?" asked Brian Halo. "What's wrong?"

The mayor brought the little screen to his face, the view from the camera jerking up from the street, to the bridge rushing in, a moment to focus, the bricks getting larger, a red wave crashing over. The mayor let out a shortened cry, the only sound he'd made that day, followed by a shortened thud overhead. The screen black. He dropped the TV and grabbed at his chest, and fell face-over on the floor.

Brian Halo picked up the little television. "We've lost the camera," he said. He pointed to the mayor, motionless on the floor, "And I believe the mayor has stopped breathing." Rob moved next to him, the two of them bending over. "This mayor is definitely not breathing," Brian Halo said. "Do you know CPR?"

"I do," Rob knelt beside the old man, rolling him over, the face that now looked like an inflated fish. Rob stood quickly, "No I don't," he said.

"Now we're stopping. Why are we stopping?" The little window to the front seat crashed open, the driver behind it. "We had a little accident."

65

Don saw the bridge pass over, the cameraman's fall, bank customers cheering as the armored car came to a stop. He climbed across to the Dahlia's trunk, kicking and pushing the men off, enough to bend down and see how the cars were connected, one bumper atop another. He tried with his hands first and gave up and stood and jumped on the trunk, three times until he felt it let go, leaping back as the Cantor shot forward.

Little Eddy was a block ahead, running as fast as when he began, but he was no match for the loose Cantor, which covered the ground between them in seconds, still picking up speed when it hit him. Eddy lying on the hood, the bag sitting by his arm.

Don crawled to the roof, reaching down, grabbing the handle as Eddy rolled over, pulling it under his chest.

"Give me the bag," Don said.

Eddy looked up to the masked man above. "Don?" he asked. "It's you, right?"

"Just give me the bag Eddy and we can let you off."

"Tell me something Don, if I were you, would I give the bag to me?"

Don didn't answer. He was looking ahead, something in the road, Eddy turning over to see, at least a dozen police cars blocking the street. "That's it, baby," said Little Eddy, "you're done."

66

Dyan Swaine waited in the doorway, a plastic assault rifle pressed in her ear, a man in a turban pressing behind, breathing his lunch in her hair. "I've been waiting for this a long time, Dyan."

"Shut up before I smack you," she said. Three scenes left and then she could go home. First, from the front, of her breaking away, running across the street, and being shot, then of her from behind and being shot, and finally of her dying in the arms of Lieutenant Gates. The prop master had attached multiple explosives to her back and chest, each connected to a silicone vial of fake blood and set to go off from a transmitter in his pocket. He said the force of the blasts would kill her if not for the bulletproof vest.

"Action," the director said, and she elbowed the turban in the ribs, pushing the rifle up, then running toward the cops, their guns firing at the terrorists. As always in these moments, she was terrified that someone had mistakenly loaded real bullets instead of blanks. Then from behind her came the trill of the assault rifle, and with it she felt the first wave of explosives firing in her back.

67

Dyan was lying on her stomach in the street, the cops in front of her, the set of *Ten Thirteen.* She was aware of that, and of the sound of a car skidding close, Dyan rolling away as it stopped. There was the sky, and a masked man flying through it, landing at her feet. More masked men appeared, one of them kneeling next to her, "Dyan, it's me, Tim," his hand gently on her forehead. "How could they do this to you." Tim put his arms under and lifted her up, fake blood over his hands and chest. "It's okay," Tim whispered, "you're gonna be okay."

She just wanted the day to end, for all of it to be over. She wrapped her arms around his neck as he carried her to the car.

68

Walter Yoshi, the director of *Ten Thirteen,* stood in the middle of the street and watched the Cantor driving away with Dyan Swaine. He looked down into his little TV, pushed a few buttons and watched the scene again, and turned to the prop master behind. "The hell with Dyan. We'll use the stand-in. Hit her in the back and skip the front shot and go right to Gates. And this time I think more bullet holes, don't you. And more blood."

"I don't know," said the prop master in his Belgian accent, "the stand-in is not so strong as Dyan." But the director had already moved on, the next set of orders. The prop master stared at the empty street, sounds of cameramen resetting the scene. He reached in his pocket and pulled out the little transmitter, the red button on the right connected to a receiver in Dyan's chest, the blood charges set to explode in the front of her shirt. "Good-bye, Dyan," he said, and pushed the button.

69

Brian Halo and Rob stood side by side watching the ambulance crew fit the body of the mayor into a stretcher. One of the paramedics punched the mayor's chest with his hands, the other punching air through a tube in the mayor's mouth.

"How's he doing?" Rob asked.

"How does it look like he's doing?" one of them said as they lifted the stretcher and sent it careening into the back of the ambulance.

Brian Halo stepped between, "He means to say do you think the mayor's going to make it?"

"Do I think he's going to make it? Hey Larry," the paramedic shouted at his partner, "do I think he's going to make it?"

"The fucking mayor for Christ sake," Larry said, the doors of the ambulance closing.

Brian Halo watched it clatter away. "I guess we can't pay him back the money then."

A second ambulance arrived and Renaldo was detached from the backseat of the Dahlia. Several of the bank customers collected at the windows, rubbing their necks as they looked on, as if the injuries to the actor might be contagious.

Anthony King and Arnold, who had escaped with minor head wounds, walked from the car to stand beside Rob. A solitary figure was approaching them, a man not much larger than a child.

"Where's the bag Eddy?" Halo said.

Eddy lifted his shirt, showing his bleached middle. "Don's got it."

King stepped forward, "I can get that bag for you, Mr. Halo."

"He's got Dyan Swaine too," Little Eddy said. "Kidnapped her from the set of *Ten Thirteen.* She had blood all over."

Brian Halo reached out for the shoulders of Arnold and Rob. He closed his eyes and performed a simple rapid-breathing exercise.

"I can take care of Don, too," said King.

"Yes, yes, yes," Halo said between breaths. He was looking the other way, back to the bridge, the cameraman limping toward them, his camera under his arm, using his tripod as a crutch.

"How's the camera?" Halo said, words taken away by the notes of a loud bass guitar, which turned out to be a broken muffler, the black Cantor coming around the block, flying up Marginal, actors and extras running for the curb, Don holding the bag out the window as they passed.

"The shot, get the shot," Halo grabbed the cameraman with two hands, shoving the lens at the Cantor. "Shoot them."

King and Arnold pulled their guns as one and began firing at the car, the bullets bouncing off parked cars and telephone poles, an abandoned welfare office.

70

Tom tried to make the left on Lemmings, the buses backed up to the bridge, forcing him east, past Low Street, locked up with garbage trucks, and Sodden shut for some kind of Chinese holiday. The rest of the roads out of Crumbtown had sunk too far and were blocked off with construction barriers and detour signs, promises of bridges that would never be built. Even Leaven Street, which Tom was sure was still open, had been chained and padlocked, a hand-painted sign in the middle, "No Way Out," leaving him no choice but to drive to the water, the weather-beaten fencing to the bottom of town, all the way around to Marginal from where they'd come. Everyone but Don ducking down as they passed the armored car and the broken Dahlia, ambulance sirens and gunshots, and when they were through, the Cantor's other four occupants raised their heads: Tom and Tim and Dyan in the front, Don and Rita in the back. "Is everyone okay?" Don asked.

"I'm all right," Dyan said. Then she exploded.

Fake blood burst from her chest like grapes out of a cannon, splattering the windshield, covering it red. "She's hit," Tim cried, and burrowed his face in her chest. Tom smeared at the glass with his hand while Don checked the windows for holes, the doors. "Strange," he said.

Tim raised his head, "It's sweet," licking the fake blood from his chin.

"Wow that hurts," said Dyan, unbuttoning her shirt. "Oh my God," said Tim.

Tom wiped at the fake blood until there was nothing to be seen of the street. "Hey Don, how much is in the bag."

"It looks like it's all here," Don said, "fifty thousand."

"Fifty G's," said Tim.

Dyan finished taking off her uniform shirt and unfastened the bulletproof vest, a white T-shirt underneath. "What's going on?" she asked, her speech slurred, still reeling from the last concussion.

"We just robbed a bank," said Tim.

Dyan smiled, "I'm going to rob banks too."

Don kept checking the rear window. "We need to get another car, one without blood all over it. And she has to leave."

"Why does she have to leave?" said Tim.

Dyan rolled up her bloodied police shirt and leaned over Tim, holding it out the window, "To Captain Palmer," she shouted, throwing it in the wind.

"Fifty G's," said Tom. "Hey Don, who's better than us?" He turned on the radio, a guitar rising in, the Cantor crossing over the bridge, into Old Dodgeport, then quickly left and left, through narrow streets along the river, under the canted shadows of concrete pillars, the packed roar of the expressway over their heads, that crumbled Crumbtown from the rest of the city. "Who's better than us?"

Twelve

SCENE 71

Tom knew a good parking lot by the train station, unguarded, the row of cars in the back never seen by the sun. He let Don out and drove over to Herman's, the other side of the river, where the four of them finished six Michigans and a double bucket of hard-boiled potatoes. Don pulled up twenty minutes later, a red Bollinger in near perfect condition. He said he wasn't going to take it, that it would attract too much attention. "You had to do it," said Tom, who loved Bollingers as much as Don.

They took Sunset out of town, past new roads made out of billboard and block, the flat earth between laced with quick malls and Internet outlets. They stopped at the farmers' market just before Hokum, and bought frozen apples and T-shirts that said "Property of Creosote Correctional" on the front. Dyan signed autographs on matchbooks, milk cartons, the backs of credit cards. Tom and Tim stood beside her and were treated like royal bodyguards, and given free sports drinks and postcards.

Don took over behind the wheel, steering with one hand on Rita's knee, the other over the radio, all the songs about girls and cars, and girls and cars. The Bollinger didn't need much attention; just keep the hood pointed at the front end, the highway on the horizon. The cars around him were like toys in comparison, the shapes of peeled vegetables.

"Where are we going?" asked Tom.

"Let's have a party," Dyan said.

"Dyan and me are going to Mexico," said Tim. "I saw it on TV, they have a town that's all bank robbers, from all over the world. They charge the tourists five dollars just to take their pictures."

"Let's go there," Dyan said.

Don had only planned for the robbery, not where they would go after. He'd been away so long, only a few days to relearn the world. It used to be the cars were square and the earth was round, and if you drove straight you could die several times before finding yourself again. Now it seemed like the country was all right angles, one leading to another, right back to the same nobody you left, same old lousy housing with a new name on the door. He didn't want to go to New York. He didn't want to know how to sail or speak Spanish or tell the difference between a maple and an elm. He didn't want to go anywhere except straight ahead with the music on and his hand in Rita's skirt, her hair blowing over his face.

"Where do you want to go?" he asked.

"Something with not so many red lights," she said.

"I know the place." He left Sunset near New Blunder and passed through two housing developments ridged around an acre of water called Seven Lake. A mile later the road narrowed and jumped quickly back and forth over a stream, the houses getting smaller until they were gone. "What're you looking for?" said Tom. "The Willow? I think it fell down."

"It fell down a few times," said Tim, "and then the town was going to knock it down after Billy's son tried to make it topless. And then that Indian guy was going to turn it into a water park, that guy who used to drink in there all the time. What was his name?"

"He wasn't really Indian," Tom said. "He told me he was adopted."

"Well it doesn't matter because it fell down again, and it used to be right here; it's not here anymore."

"It was never here," said Tom. "I think we passed it."

"No look. The dead trees; it's down there."

Don almost lost control on the steep curve, the dry wheels calling out to the bare trees killed by the bumpers of men staggering out of the bar. At the bottom of the turn the old Willow leaned over them just the same as he remembered, like it had rolled there from the top of the hill, neon script leaking out of the cracks in the walls. The place was always more an idea anyway, which somebody had about where the world should end and start again. They used to drive out there after jobs, sleep upstairs with Mother Time and her dogs. Even then, when he'd be drunk two or three days at once, he couldn't say for certain that the place existed.

He pulled the Bollinger into the rocky drive and turned off the car radio; all of them waiting as the pitying words of Hank Williams slowly made their way across the lot, into the open windows of the car.

"It's wonderful," said Dyan.

Tom and Tim each grabbed a handful of bills from the bag and wrestled Dyan to the top of the stairs, where she twisted off a part of the front door. "It's so real I love it," she said.

"Just don't touch anything inside," Tim put his arm in her elbow, "except me."

72

Walking into the Willow with Dyan Swaine at his side, and more money in his hand than he could spend, was for Tim the end of every dream he'd ever had. Of course he might have changed a few details, added a limousine, and a large crowd inside, and a bartender who wasn't a wrecked Costa Rican prostitute named Ingrid who'd once threatened to bite off his ear, but these were only the dream's accessories. The two essential elements, the girl and the money, were what mattered most, and this night Tim had the best of both. It was almost as if he were already at the bar, watching himself walk through the doors, a beautiful actress on his arm, Tim thinking, Here was the man he'd always imagined himself to be, despite so many years of evidence to the contrary. He wished Loretta could see this.

Tom slammed the door behind them, forcing a lit beer sign to the floor. The men at the bar cocked their heads to the sound, finally opening their eyes when they saw Dyan. The bartender refused to look. People had been calling her Ingrid for over forty years and she never forgot a debt. "You better be holding twenty-seven bucks, Tim Dwight," she said without noticeably moving her lips, "or you and Tom can take the gas."

Tim dragged Dyan toward the bar and floated down a single bill. "Sorry Ingrid, but all I've got is hundreds. Get yourself something, and for my friends here." He pulled out another.

"And I'll give one of these Franklins to anybody who can take a picture of me and my girl here. We're getting married next week."

Everyone remained silent while Ingrid examined the bill, holding it under three different lights before wedging it into her girdle, the men suddenly talking at once, Tim's voice yelling above the rest. "Drinks on me, *cabrones*."

It was one of Tim's finest performances. He ordered beer in German, and tequila in Mexican. He sang three verses of "Your Cheating Heart" and then asked Ingrid to raise her skirt. When the men had effectively surrounded Dyan, he pulled her free, whirling through a free-associating series of dance moves, the cha-cha, flamenco, and rumba, the mooch and the sugarfoot, and then he sat down, exhausted, Dyan pulling at his arms, trying to get him to stand. "Give us a minute, baby," he said, "to have a few cigarettes." He looked around the room, realizing nobody was listening, that he'd been invisible for some time.

They'd seen nothing but her since he walked in the door—each man taking a different part, watching with half breaths, like they were unable to look at the whole and would put the pieces together later, over the years to come. "Who wants to dance?" she shouted, and waited while their eyes disappeared under a collective brow, like they were trying to answer a riddle. Dyan shrugged and looked over to Don and Rita, who for several minutes had been stuck in the corner. Then she climbed a stool to the bar and shook her hands and clapped her hips. It didn't matter that she couldn't dance. "Come on guys, let's party."

Warner Hotel was the de facto leader of the group. He'd

worked as a box cutter in Alaska and had once been hit by lightning, and so with great fanfare he stepped up to the rail and batted all bottles and glasses to the floor. Then he pulled himself to a seat on the bar and stretched to his back, looking up, Dyan dancing over him. He smiled and the rest of the men cheered.

"What's wrong with you guys," she waved her arms. "Get up and dance with me. Come on. Life is short."

"Oh no baby," Ingrid corrected. "Life is no short. Life is tall." She leaned over and dropped a fistful of bourbon into Warner Hotel's mouth, closing it with her hand, shaking it down.

Tim stuffed his cigarette into the floor and shouted, "I'll dance with you." He climbed the stool to the bar and grabbed her hand. "I'd eat the moon for you, Dyan," and twirled her around his glass.

"Go, go, go," Warner banged his elbows on the bar. He'd never seen Dyan Swaine from this angle before, and wondered if maybe he was the first person to do so. She wasn't as beautiful this way, but man was she big. He couldn't wait to tell his wife, who was always complaining about him wasting his time at the bar.

73

Rita felt Don's arm cross under her, his hands growing on her hip as they walked across the lot, climbing the nail-filled stairs to the top. When Don closed the bar door the lights went off, the frazzled guitar getting louder in the dark, turning them into each other, three steps past the jukebox, the pool table, breathing in the corner, "I can't leave you anymore," she said.

"Okay," he mumbled, and they agreed that was enough talking. Their lips came together briefly. "If you could go anywhere," Don asked, "where would you be?" He moved his hands under her shirt, spreading the muscles down her back. Hank Williams began another song about divorce.

"Havana," she said.

"I mean somewhere we can drive to."

"Mexico City," she breathed, his ear on her lips.

"Crossing the border's too risky. I'm talking about in the United States." His finger circled a mole on her hip. She raised his shirt to his navel, "We passed that motel in the road. The Las Vegas," she said, "I would like a place called the Las Vegas." He let go of her back, she grabbed his hands as if he might fall. "We can stay here, too," he said. "They used to have a room upstairs. There was a couch and a rug and the door locks . . ."

"Anywhere," she said.

Dyan and Tim danced slowly next to the jukebox, their bodies bumping into it like ships against a dock, making the records skip. She was so drunk she had to dance on her toes to feel the floor. "Look out," she said as the floor dropped again, clinging to him as if he were holding her from a trapeze. "What was in that drink?"

"It's a crumbsoda," Tim said. "All the white liquors are there, gin, vodka, tequila, rum, and triple sec, and some cola for color."

. . .

Tom leaned over the bar and banged his bottle against the sink. "Hey Ingrid, put on channel 63, *The Brian Halo Show*, it starts in five minutes. He's making a TV show about when we used to rob banks."

"And more drinks for everyone, right?" said the man next to Tom, whose name had something to do with cannons.

"That's right," Tom said.

"Cost you fifty bucks to change the channel," Ingrid said.

"Fifty bucks? You used to charge a dollar."

"The Sox are on."

"Forget the goddamn Red Sox, Ingrid. Here's a dollar to change the channel. Been watching the Sox lose my whole goddamn life. That's why I'm getting out."

"Don't go," the man next to him said. "Please stay."

"I crashed my father's car the night we lost the tiebreaker," Tom said. "Nineteen seventy-eight. I was in the hospital for eight weeks."

"My wife stopped talking to me after '86," said another man, his face riddled with toothpicks. "Up by two runs in the bottom of the ninth. One out left to win the whole thing. Hasn't said a word to me in fifteen years."

"It ain't like the old days, though," said the old man at the bar's end, his hat cleaned of all color. "My father died after the impossible-dream season, '67. Heart attack in the last game of the series, after they lost to Gibson for the third time. Survived Guadalcanal, and the goddamn Red Sox killed him."

"Well they're not gonna get me," said Tom, "because we're leaving, baby, and we're going where nobody ever heard of the

Boston Goddamn Red Sox. Now come on Ingrid, turn the channel."

"One hundred bucks," said Ingrid.

74

The Brian Halo Show opened the same as always, a spinning helicopter shot of Manhattan night, cutting to a limousine heading south on Seventh Avenue, to stop at a world-famous alleyway, the velvet doors opening, the thumping of lights within, a blinding face-filled din as one beautiful person after another yelled "Hi Brian" to the lens. The show then cut through a montage of parties: a political fund-raiser in a downtown cathedral, a soup kitchen benefit on a Miami schooner, a PTA meeting in a Beverly Hills pool hall. Each scene had been crowded with the most popular people, from every walk of life, all of them speaking bluntly of why they loved Brian Halo, the sequence ending with model Susan Klee saying, "Because he's the only person I can talk to about sex."

This Friday, however, the opening went beyond Ms. Klee, the camera "eye" traveling to one more showcase, a short city street adrift with red emergency lights, the former child actor Little Eddy standing next to a police car, Brian Halo's hand on his shoulder. "There's no party here, folks, no movie premieres, only police lights. Tonight we're coming to you from the little city of Dodgeport, where a stunning tragedy has just taken place."

To a backdrop of carefully chosen cuts from the day's

shooting, Brian Halo described the crash, the robbery, the valiant efforts of Little Eddy as well as the other actors and homeless men who worked together in vain to retrieve the money. He provided a moving elegy to the mayor of the city, who had had a heart attack during the shooting, a man who lost his life for giving, the segment ending with footage from *Ten Thirteen,* describing how the robbers kidnapped Ms. Dyan Swaine. A ten-minute tribute followed the commercial, Dyan's work on *Ten Thirteen,* as well as cover shots from major TV magazines, pictures of Dyan at parties, the famous hotel shower shots of the French paparazzi.

75

Five minutes after *The Brian Halo Show* began, Ingrid cut off the jukebox and turned up the television volume. By the time Don's picture was shown at the end, with a description of the ten-thousand-dollar reward, a phone number to call for information, the men at the bar were giving it all the attention they had.

"Damn," said Tim, who'd watched the show with Dyan sleep-dancing on his shoulder. "Uncle Maury died. We should have a drink for Maury."

"We should leave now," said Tom, pointing to the men around them, all heading to the pay phone.

"Oh come on Tom, these guys wouldn't turn us in." One of the men came and asked for a quarter, then took his place in the line that now ran from the phone to the bathroom.

"We have to go," Tom whispered, pointing to Warner Hotel

blocking the front door. "And we need to tell Don and Rita. I think they went upstairs."

Dyan Swaine lifted her head from Tim's neck, "They tied me up in the back of a store," she said, "going to shoot me in the street," splicing her day together from the three crumb-sodas she'd drunk, and the two explosions earlier, in her chest and back, which made it hard for her to see objects on her right. "Two months they wouldn't give me any lunch."

"Filthy men," Ingrid said. She pulled a lead-filled baton from under the bar and waved it at Tom's head. "I hope they fry you up for this."

76

Don led Rita up the stairs and down the hall, the room in the back smelling like an old tree fort, of pine and pee and wet porno magazines. The same jukebox songs were playing there, two speakers in the wall nearly as loud as in the bar, but with only half the anguish. Hank Williams started to sing, "I'll never get out of this world alive," as Don reached out blindly for the Creosote logo on Rita's shirt, his fingers reading each letter twice. So happy to be free of last night's hooks and buttons that he took his time going underneath, around her hips first, then up to her shoulders and back, unsnapping her bra on the third pass. Slowly, he guided both hands forward, going further under and finding himself pushed off the couch, sitting on the carpet, Rita standing over. "Watch carefully," she said, turning her hands back and forth, as if about to do a trick, then in one quick move she reached in her sleeve and pulled out the bra, holding it like a rabbit by the ears. Don climbed to his knees to her breasts loose under her shirt, her nipples growing up in the lines of his palm.

There was no rush, time had broken. The only clock in the world was his hand lifting up her shirt, which at the rate it was going might take hours to take it off. Because for the first time in a long time, longer than he could remember, he didn't want to be anywhere else, didn't want to be anyone else. What else did you call that except happy; he was happy; everything here was for them. She had a little mole next to her navel, round and brown, and he'd spent the past several minutes kissing her there, the navel to the mole and back again, the out to the in, the beginning to the end. "Come here," she finally said, and pulled his mouth back to hers, her hands rappelling to his hips and, with a deafening click, unsnapping his pants. "Havana," he said. Followed by another click as Tim and Tom and Dyan burst in.

"We got a problem," Tom said.

77

King and Arnold waited in the front of an unmarked '98 Hurricane police cruiser. They wore new police uniforms, with new haircuts and makeup to accentuate their policelike earnestness. Behind the Hurricane, Rob Landetta and Brian Halo held up sheets between their outstretched arms, to improvise the walls of a dressing room in which Little Eddy stood, in boxer shorts and police uniform socks, his hands out to ward off the wardrobe assistants, the lineup of police pants they'd brought.

"I don't understand," Eddy said. "Why I have to be a cop?"

Rob stepped forward, "Just put the pants on, Eddy. We're going live in two minutes."

"Shut up, Rob," Brian Halo said. "I'm directing now." He turned to Eddy and began nodding aggressively, "You've been robbed, Eddy. These people have been robbed. Dyan Swaine, one of the most popular actresses on the planet, has been kidnapped. This is about justice. Now please put the pants on."

Eddy grabbed the pants and then pushed them back, "Look, I don't got to hide behind no badge, man. I can take care of Don, no cameras, no backup, just me and him, that's all I'm asking."

"Eddy, Eddy, listen to me. Rob here had this idea of making a crime show without cops, and I think it's pretty clear from the mess we have here why we need cops in a crime show, okay. It's important that you put this on so that people will see you as the moral authority here, as a symbol of order, so that the people will see that the system still works."

Eddy put one foot into his pants. "Nobody gets away with robbing me." He hopped several times on one leg, "I want Don myself, I want him," hopping until he fell on the Hurricane, punching the trunk with his forehead.

"Help him, Rob, what's wrong with you?" Halo said. "It's okay Eddy, you'll get Don, don't worry. For all of us, and for your father, too."

"My father?"

"Your father on *The Two of Us*. Sergeant Chryton Langdon, NYPD. I think he'd be pretty proud right now, to see you in that uniform."

"I think he'd be very drunk right now."

"He was a good father, Eddy, and a good cop, too, maybe

the best TV cop of all time, am I right? So who better than you to take his place?"

Eddy battered in the buttons on his police shirt. "If I messed up my lines he used to beat the shit out of me."

"But on that screen, Eddy, he was the best, and no one can ever take that from him. Everybody's going to want to see how you handle the job. There's some pressure on you. Especially as you are going to be starting off as a lieutenant."

Brian Halo held out the gold bars for the wardrobe assistant to pin on. "A lieutenant?" Eddy said, nodding his head.

"There's something else I have to tell you. I didn't want you to get too upset but the truth is that Dyan Swaine is your partner, Eddy, for years now. They kidnapped your partner."

Eddy grabbed his own hair with two hands and pulled up until he was standing on his toes. "My partner." One of the wardrobe assistants bent down to buckle the police belt, adjust the holster, Eddy jumped backward, shouting "Freeze." He walked over to the Hurricane and retrieved his nine-millimeter pistol from the pile of clothes on the hood. He checked the clip. "Cops thrive on pressure, Brian. That's the one thing I have in common with cops."

Rob stepped forward, "We're going live in one minute."

Eddy holstered the gun and patted it, "If you think about it, my study of Don was only to help prepare me for this role of catching Don. I know what he thinks, I know what he wants. I may be the only one who can find him."

78

Tim closed the door and pushed his back to it, shouting to Tom and Don to slide the couch up because the lock wasn't going to hold. The voices of men coming up the stairs, turning their fists against the door, all arguing over who would get the reward. Then the bludgeoning of Ingrid's baton, her relentless accent, a mix of German and Costa Rican, "Let that woman go before I break this door and then you pay for it." Her enormous hand twisting the knob. "I am getting the key you just wait."

Tim and Tom moved the couch to the door, Don still tying his shoes on one end, Rita trying to put her bra on under her shirt. Dyan sat down between them, her eyes closed, she began to snore.

Tom climbed out the window and along the gutter to the end where a fallen tree made a drunken ladder to the ground. Don helped Rita out and they held hands on the roof's edge, waiting for Tom to bring up the car. Sirens began from somewhere far above, as if from a police plane, then suddenly loud and close as the red lights of the Hurricane appeared atop the hill, twisting toward them. Tom parked under the window and Don and Rita let themselves down to the hood.

"Maury's dead," Tom said. "He had a heart attack or something when we robbed the bank. We just saw it on the news."

"Then we can go to the Gail," Don said. "We'll be safe there."

"What's the Gail?" Rita asked.

"It's a secret house, up in the woods. Maury built it in case the feds caught up to him, or the Libyans."

"No one knows where it is," Tom said, "or if it exists."

"I've been there. Just take 25 North. I'll tell you."

Tim grabbed Dyan's hands, "Come on," pulling her off the couch, her arm over his shoulder as he led her to the window.

"Where are we going?"

A truck turned into the lot, a camera crew on its roof, and with it, Ingrid's voice rushing up from the bar, "Hey boys, we're on TV. Come down to here and look." The men forgetting about the door, rushing downstairs to see.

Dyan was halfway out when she heard the noise. "TV?" she cried. "We're on TV? Where?" She climbed back into the room, pointing to the old television in the corner. "Let's see."

"Come on Dyan, we have to go."

"Wait." She stumbled to the television, switched it on, the bar shaking itself onto the screen, the view from the camera crew bouncing into the parking lot. "Oh look, there's the bar, and look in the window there is me and you watching TV."

Tim pulled at her arm. "Come on, Dyan."

"Oh no I can't go out like this. I'm too drunk to go out there." She tried to pull away. He lifted her over his shoulder and climbed out the window. "They think that we kidnapped you."

"Kidnapped?" she shouted, grabbing the frame with two hands. "No way am I getting kidnapped again," fighting to pull herself back in, "let me go." She kicked him in the stomach, Tim slipping off the gutter, clutching her belt, Dyan holding them both from the sill. "Let go of me."

"Let go of her," Tom shouted from the car below, "and get in."

"She wants to come," said Tim. "I want her to come."

Dyan pulled her head above the sill and looked back to the TV in the corner, the picture of outside the bar, of Tim sliding down her leg. "Oh my God," she said, "look how big my butt is."

79

The Hurricane's siren died painfully, three men in their uniforms getting out, crouching behind the open doors, guns drawn. Little Eddy called into his loudspeaker, "This is the cops. Drop your weapons and put your hands on your heads." He lowered the mike and leaned forward, "Let's not shoot the hostage unless we have to."

The back doors of the camera truck opened and a camera crew marched out, assembling in a line in front of Rob Landetta. "I want you to set up about twenty feet ahead of Eddy," Rob said, "so that it looks like his gun is pointed at the camera."

"Not me," said the cameraman, his head still bandaged from being knocked off the truck. "Eddy already shot that one actor."

"It's okay, we put blanks in the gun."

"What about the other two," the man said. "We're not doing it." He put down his camera and walked back to the van, the rest of them watching. Then the cameraman's assistant stepped forward and picked up the camera.

"You got the job," Rob said. "Okay men, stay low," and the

group charged forward, getting in line on their knees in front of the police car.

Little Eddy stood with his gun pointing through the car window, over the heads of the crew, the way thousands of cops had done it before. "Hold your fire," Eddy said, blinking repeatedly through the sights. There was Dyan hanging from the window, Tim holding on to her police belt, which had slipped to her knees. "Not yet," Eddy said, watching the belt slide to her ankles, her shoes, sliding over. Tim fell to the car below, up on his knees on the hood. "The hostage is free," Eddy screamed. "Take them out."

Dyan heard the gunfire behind and closed her eyes, waiting for the explosives in her back, the second time she'd been shot at in one day. Then the sill broke off in her hand and she slid down the roof and over the gutter, ten feet to the ground, crawling to the car. Five hundred thousand dollars was not enough for this. More shots followed, Little Eddy shouting "Cease-fire" as she climbed into the seat beside Tim, down to the floor at his feet, where Tom was squeezing into her bulletproof vest.

"Give me that," she said.

80

Brian Halo watched the show from his command truck, parked on top of the hill. In the back were phones stacked on computers, two technicians sitting before a bank of three televisions. Screen One was from the camera he'd stationed outside his truck, a wide view of the bar below, the Bollinger and the Hurricane in the lot. Screen Two was from the camera truck at the edge of the lot, a close-up of Dyan and Tim getting into the Bollinger. Screen Three was empty.

"What happened to Three?" Halo yelled. "The close-up of Eddy. Where's my cops?" He turned to Screen Two, the Bollinger's lights driving out of the lot. "They're getting away. I need Three."

"There he is," the technician pointed to Screen One, zooming in to the cameraman's assistant, sitting on the ground in front of the police cruiser, holding the pieces of Camera Three.

"Three's been hit," the technician said.

Halo turned to Screen Two, the shot of the Bollinger leaving up the hill, driving toward the command truck. Halo banged on the front wall of the truck. "Driver," he shouted, "block off the road. We'll turn them around up here." He grabbed the headset of one of the technicians, the head still attached, "Camera Two, get in the back of the police car. You can shoot them coming down the hill."

He searched the papers on the counter, finding his map of Greater Dodgeport, the thin red line of the road they were on, tracing it with his finger, all the way back to where it met the expressway, the western edge of the city. He'd chase them down there, get some lighting trucks set up, a proper blockade, the fireworks to end the chase. The biggest television story in months and *The Brian Halo Show* was right in front. Exactly the kind of major event that could catapult a program, get him out of the local access market, land him on one of the nationals. *The Real Adventures of Robin and Rita* was finished. With the mayor dead, so was the backing. Brian Halo was the mayor now. This was his show.

He looked over to Screen One, the Bollinger coming up the hill, to stop before the command truck, turning around. He turned to Screen Two, the cameraman in back of the police cruiser, pulling out of the lot, into the road, Eddy's head at the wheel, eclipsed by the lights coming down. "Go to Two," Halo said. "We'll get the shot driving past. Then turn around and start the chase." The oncoming headlights of the Bollinger merging into one, quickly filling the screen, driving at the lens. Halo picked up the microphone under the counter, the radio for the police cruiser, "Lieutenant Eddy? What are you doing? Get out of the way." A cry of skidding tires, Eddy swerving at the last moment, the Bollinger passing, lights flying away as if taken by the wind, the sound of a cameraman's scream, the scraping of dead branches, then nothing. "What happened?"

"We lost Two," the technician said.

Thirteen

SCENE 81

Rita lay on the backseat, the moon chasing them through the rear glass, trees eating away the bottom rows of stars. Don rested on top of her, his head curled over her chest, knees bent between. He hadn't moved or spoken since the shooting started, how long that was she couldn't remember, with the weight of him, the road pushing up from beneath, like she was floating, and when they stopped, she'd disappear. He raised his head as if to speak, then suddenly pushing off her, looking through the window, "I don't see anything," he said. "I think we're clear."

He stared out at the trees falling behind, hills flattening in the dark, like a black curtain sweeping forward. On the curve ahead a lone street lamp came toward them, its light flipping over, the floor to the roof to the backseat, holding to her face. For a moment she was almost too bright, the picture of the first time he'd seen her, then it was gone, a blanket on them together. The race was ending, he could feel it, like he was both still in it and at the same time already finished, a part of him sitting on the hill, watching them drive away. What happened before didn't matter, all forgotten, the hopes and failures, escapes and jail terms, like the room for his memory had shrunk to a trunk, a few pictures locked up, the key always getting stuck. There was only the finish to think about, the end the only way out, a kiss and lights off, sitting in the dark, alone with their own ever-after.

When they got to the Gail he'd send off the others. Split the money outside, a bigger cut for the twins if they promised to find another continent. Then he'd light a fire, a bottle of wine from the basement, lying with Rita on a blanket on the floor, the long night of slowing down. They'd learn how to write the words for themselves, no cameras, no scripts, it would be more like the books he used to take out from the library in prison, which he could never finish, with ten pages for breakfast, a whole chapter on toes, too boring to read unless you were in it, the details of living, moment to moment. He reached down through the dark to find her arms, her shoulders to her face, her eyes finding his, telling him they were going to win. "Kiss me," she said, and he did, his hands to her back, the wheels underneath.

82

Tim reached down to the floor of the car where Dyan was sitting, "We lost them," he said, and grabbed her hand, pulling her to the seat. She looked through the windshield, at the road swelling under the lights, then back to the dark hem of the hill behind, Don and Rita kissing in the back. "Oh why don't they just give up," she said.

Tim held her by the head. "They're cops, baby, that's what they do."

"I mean these two right here, it's disgusting," she pointed to the bench seat below, Rita now on top of Don, all their hearing gone.

"Me and Loretta used to be like that. My ex, when we first met we had to kiss everywhere we went. For about a year and a half. I think that's why she hates me so much."

"You should never show it," Dyan said, "if you really love someone, because once other people see, then it's not yours anymore. It's just like everything else." Her blond hair turned red as she finished, red spreading to the rest of the car, a police siren behind, knocking at the windows, calling their names, tim-tom, tim-tom, the Hurricane again. "Like this stupid car chase," she said, "that's never going to end."

"Here they come," said Tim. "Faster."

Tom sat alone with the wheel. They were going the wrong way, back to Dodgeport. He wanted to tell them. He didn't know what to do. "I've never been in love," he cried, his eyes so wet he could barely stay on the road, swerving left as the Hurricane passed on the right, its lights disappearing ahead.

83

"What are you doing?" said King. "You just passed them. Now they're behind."

Eddy squinted at the Hurricane's windshield, "Where are my lights?"

"They're on," said King. "Tell me the truth, you ever drive a car before."

Eddy should have let someone else take the wheel, once they'd pushed the car from the ditch. He didn't like driving at night, especially without his glasses, but it was important to set a good example, that he was a strong leader, a man to rely on in a crisis. Sure there were times when he became a little anxious, when he needed some help to get through, the world so hard sometimes he had to squeeze his heart faster just to know it was still there. Yes, Little Eddy really badly needed some cocaine right now, but Lieutenant Eddy was focused. This lieutenant could act. He just needed more light.

"I said behind us, man." King grabbed Eddy's head and pointed it at the rearview mirror, the blinking white eyes of the Bollinger. "Slow down and let them pass you, the roadblock's all set up, maybe three miles."

"I can't see," Eddy waved his hand at the dash. He reached down and turned off the lights.

"Oh no," said Arnold.

Brian Halo's voice burst out of the speaker near Eddy's knee. "Turn on your lights Lieutenant Eddy. Do you read me? Turn on your lights immediately and pull over and let them pass you and then proceed to chase. Do you copy?"

Eddy picked up the microphone and said, "Ten-4. We'll shoot them as they go by."

"That's a negative, Lieutenant. You are to follow the perpetrators to the roadblock. You are not to pass them on the way. You are not to shoot them on the way. At the roadblock you will be assisting the police unit on the scene, Detective Hammamann, in making the arrest. Due to the nature of the hostage situation, you will not fire unless fired upon. Is that understood?"

"Ten-4," Eddy shook his head at the ceiling, "I can't chase 'em. And I can't shoot 'em. Okay so tell me what I'm doing here." He dropped the microphone and pulled out his gun. "This is not why I became a cop." He hit the brakes with two feet.

84

A pair of taillights broke red in the empty darkness fifty feet away. Tom stuck the brake to the floor and cut the wheel all the way left, the car suddenly lighter, the brakes still locked, sliding straight ahead, twenty feet, ten. He let go of the pedal, the front tires catching, everything jumping left, just clearing the Hurricane's back bumper, then right, just missing the front, then round in a circle, five hundred and forty degrees.

Tim quit trying to hold Dyan, who'd been screaming since the skid began. He looked out the windshield, the headlights behind them. "I turn away for two seconds," he said, "and you start driving backwards."

Tom hit the brakes again, spinning the wheel, the car going forward now, his foot on the gas, two miles downhill to the edge of Dodgeport, with the ramps to the expressway blocked off, cross streets locked with cops, and nowhere for Tom to go but under and left along the water, up over a short ridge, three police cars wedged between the pillars on the other side, lighting trucks cutting off any chance of turning around, the road lit up like a stock car race. "Hold on," he said.

85

It was like ten years ago, Rita thought, like she was still in high school, always kissing in the smallest places, with the most people around, kissing without a beginning or an end, just that ache in the middle she once imagined sex would be like. And here almost thirty years old and kissing like a virgin again, a virgin who'd found out exactly what that ache was, and how fast the end could come, and now all she wanted was to touch him, only to get on top while she tasted his smell, of his neck and chest and under his arms, behind his ear, her lips closed tight over the words coming up, that she didn't want to let out, but there they were, and all she did was breathe, "I love you."

She jerked her head back, hitting the ceiling, hands reaching out to cover his face, as if to stop what she'd just said from going in. "Do not say," she said. "It is not love. Passions, yes. But we have just met. Do not say it back. Kiss."

Her eyes closed, her breath on his lips. She'd said that she loved him, I love you she said. The first time ever that someone said that to him, or the first time he listened. The car made a sharp turn, Don's feet against the door, legs riding up, the headlights above. He was going to tell her. Shh, she said, a white fire in her hair, lights bursting into day, brighter than a stadium, the walls of a prison break. "I love you," he said, the words taken by a scream, a woman in the front seat, gunshots outside, bullets on the car. "What's going on?" He pushed her to the side, sitting up to see.

86

Detective Hammamann thought it was the best roadblock he'd ever seen, a textbook roadblock, with the added help of the expressway pillars standing between each car, the light trucks preventing any sudden U-turns. The only weakness he could find was in the personnel on the scene: professional actors, mostly, a few extras. Of course he could have the best cops in the world there and it would still be a weakness. Because no matter how well you may think you know a person, and trust a person, you can never be sure how they're going to act when the fire flies. Simple human nature, the most complicated thing in the world.

"What do I do if they don't stop, Detective?" said the cop standing behind the car next door.

"They're going to stop, Shawn," Hammamann said. "They have no choice, okay. You just hold your position like I told you." Shawn was the only actor on the scene who'd never played a cop, one of the reasons Hammamann was keeping him close by.

"Okay, Shawn, here they come." The headlights of the Bollinger lowered atop the hill, what looked like Tom at the wheel, Tim in the passenger seat. "Ready everyone. Steady, Shawn," as the car jumped down.

Harry had been out on the pistol range most of the day, missing out on the robbery, the chase from Ingrid's bar, his recent loss of accuracy concerning him more, his own difficulties under fire, in proving his love for Loretta. He'd won her on paper, love letters and poetry, but paper wasn't going to keep Loretta. I love you, he kept saying before hitting the targets. He never missed. I love you Loretta. Why wasn't that enough?

"I'm scared, Harry," Shawn said.

"It's going to be okay, kid."

"I can't stay," said Shawn, "this is not why I became an actor."

"It's okay," Harry said. What else was there to say? He needed to concentrate on the target. The kid was gone anyway. Harry knew that all along. "Just don't take the car, Shawn." But of course he was taking the car, evacuating the lineup at the worst moment, with no time to try to close it. The Bollinger never slowed, through the gap, Harry shooting at Tim first, then the tires as they passed. Wildly off the mark.

He turned to see the Hurricane cresting the hill, Eddy driving for the break in the blockade. Harry saw Eddy's face behind the wheel. It was only a moment, but that was enough. Harry began to run. Call it police instinct, or just luck, because without warning or reason, Eddy suddenly swerved left, away from the opening, directly into the passenger door of the detective's brand-new Palais Royale.

87

The Hurricane deployed all its air bags in the crash, mushrooming them in a circle around the interior. Little Eddy's air bag pinned him to the back of his seat, then refused to deflate, leaving nothing to be seen of his face.

Detective Hammamann stood with Arnold and King at the driver's-side door. He bent in and checked Eddy's pulse, and put his ear to the white vinyl balloon. "He's talking," Hammamann said, "but I can't understand what he's saying."

A gunshot ended everything abruptly, Eddy's air bag deflating, his gun smoking in his hand, words echoing under the expressway. "I have to go to the bathroom."

88

"Fantastic," said Brian Halo. "Play that again." He stood in front of Screen Four with Rob and the technician, the three of them watching the crash repeated.

"Okay," Halo said, "let's run Three one more time and then Four once more and then go to the headlights driving away and that's a wrap. I'm starving."

"But they're getting away," said Rob. "And they've got the money. They've got Dyan."

"Where can they go, Rob?" Halo pointed to Screen Four, the retreating taillights of the Bollinger, crossing the low bridge down to Lemmings Avenue, the crumblights at the bottom of the city.

89

Don sat at the edge of the backseat, eyes out the window, the streets he grew up in, betting parlors and dollar stores and churches for rent, Crumbtown again. "How did we get back here?"

"We were heading north," said Tim, "then we got turned around."

"They blocked off the highway," Tom said. "I didn't know where else to go."

Dyan sat between them, fixing her shirt, hair sprawled over her face, "Just drop me at my hotel," she said, "anywhere, right here would be fine."

Don was still waiting for the words to explain—if this had been anyone else's story he wouldn't believe, after all that had happened, that nothing had happened. The same old broken houses with their sinking basements, secondhand curtains, borrowed lights, voices standing at the kitchen table, I am trapped here don't you understand. He punched the door, the back of the seat.

Tim changed his hat back into a mask, covering the eye-holes with his hands. "Don't hit me, Don."

"There's a store," Dyan pointed. "I'll get off here, there's a phone."

Tom parked the car under the awning's damp light, a yellow glaze creeping over the hood: Lottery Tickets, Cigarettes, Cold Beer. He opened the door. "Don't worry, Don, nobody followed us over the bridge. I'll get some sandwiches, we can crash at Louie's again."

Dyan reached for the handle, crawling over Tim, the phone outside the store. "Look at that," she said, "it's the same store they were holding me hostage in." The same store that had been surrounded by cops and cameras that afternoon, where Don had bought condoms and a six-pack the night before. "I didn't know it was a real store."

Tim reached the sidewalk, "I'll come with you," standing next to Dyan at the pay phone, pointing at the store owner in the window. "This is the guy who was holding you hostage?"

She dropped a quarter into the phone, waiting for it to ring, her hand over the receiver, "This has been a really important day for me, for what it's saying to me. That I have to go to LA, which is like what everyone's been saying: Dyan, you have to go to LA. Hello," she said to the phone, "Red Army Taxi?"

"I'm going with you," Tim said, "right after I talk to this guy." He held the door for his brother.

90

Rita sat on the other end, the seat stretched between. She tried to move closer, the space getting longer. "It is okay. We can go to my apartment. This time I do not leave."

He spread his hands on the window, metal doors across the street, "You see that, Rita, you see where we are," he did not look over. "Nothing's changed."

She thought of the moments they'd been together, dancing in the bar, driving in the car, when it seemed as if they'd known each other for years. And then moments like now, when he was more like a photograph she'd found with a name on the back, or a face drawn on a slip of money. "Okay," she said. "Nothing is changed."

She wanted her bed, a shower, and clean clothes. His hand touched her arm, "Rita I didn't mean that," like he'd been sitting next to her the whole time. "With you I'm alive." He turned her cheek, her mouth into his, falling again as the shooting began. Two gunshots in the store, then two more, reports banging on the car door.

Don stood on his knees, the bag with the money and the gun. "Stay right here," opening the door. "Don't get out of the car." Then he was gone.

91

Tom sat on a rack of broken lollipops and spilled gum, elbows bent forward over his stomach, his bloody blue shirt. Tim crouched in the aisle in the back, pointing with his rusted gun, clicking away uselessly to where the store owner was standing, the same man who'd sold Don condoms the night before, now shooting at Tim like he was handing out the change, a .22 automatic no bigger than a pack of cigarettes.

"Stop," Don shouted, pushing his gun out of the bag. "We're leaving," his best bank robber's voice, "don't," even as the store owner turned, his eyes recognizing Don a moment, then the gun jumped in the man's hand, the bullet parting Don's hair, a fly going through his ear, and just like that he shot the man in the head.

"Oh no," Don groaned, watching the man fall. He walked around the row of little pies to the untended floor behind the register, the man lying neatly in the long square, the size of his coffin, blood already to the edges, like someone pouring it out of a vase.

Tim lifted his brother, his arm under Tom's shoulder, dragging him to the door. "Don come on."

Don bent down, the man had stopped breathing but his eyes were still open, staring straight up, past the rows of prophylactics to the corner of the ceiling where a tiny video camera stared back. Don stood up to the lens, watching himself step forward over the man, the gun rising over his head. He pulled the trigger until the camera was gone. He turned to the voice behind him, the TV on the counter, Don's face on the screen, a mug shot from the first time he'd been arrested—

the words printed underneath, "Armed and Dangerous," it said, "$10,000 Reward for Capture," then a commercial, a song about hair loss. He shot the TV, the screen exploding, the song still in his head. He looked out the window, at the sound of tires on the street, Tim and Tom driving away. He ran outside, the first drops of rain hitting him in the eye. "Rita."

92

"Oh my God," Dyan cried to the phone, "the man in the store." The door crashed out, Tim grabbing her by the waist, one arm around his brother, one arm driving her to the car, shoving her into the front. Tom fell into the back, on top of Rita, pinning her to the seat, "Where is Don?"

Tim turned the key, banging on the wheel three times, "Come on come come on," banging the gears into drive, his other hand holding Dyan. Don standing in the store window, shooting at something on the counter. "What's he doing? Come on," Tim's foot off the brake, he couldn't stop it, down on the gas. "Wait," Rita shouted, pushing Tom off her. "He's still inside." She opened the door, leaning out in the rain, the street spraying away from her feet; she was going to jump.

Tim slapped the wheel around the corner, "He's coming, Rita," the door swinging in, slamming her head to the floor. "He'll meet us at the bar."

"Stop the car now," she said in Russian, pulling Tim's arm, the car bouncing off a sport utility, into another turn.

"He said he'd meet us at the bar. Right, Tom?"

Tom had pulled off his shirt and was busy squeezing it over his stomach, trying to force the blood back into the hole.

When the shirt was wrung dry he put his hand over the wound, blood still running out. He pushed his pinkie in, up to the knuckle.

"Let me out," Dyan said. "Please I won't tell, just let me go," breaking her arm free, reaching for the door as the locks dropped shut.

"I can't do that," said Tim.

Rita sat in the back, rain on the window, the red car shooting down the block. She spread her arms to where he'd just been.

ACT V

Fourteen

SCENE 93

Harry Hammamann stopped at the store's entrance, three homicide detectives inside, already working the floor, forceps and Kleenex, bags of spent shells and chewed gum. They were real cops, like Harry used to be, before he joined the mayor's department of television, five years now with the MDT. He walked in, nearly stepping in the blood in the aisle, lollipops and candied corn. Over the counter by the register he could see the coroner's mustache bobbing up and down, like he was digging a hole back there, the body on the floor. Harry didn't want to see it. He hated these scenes, the reason he left Patrol to take the job with TV. Not the sights so much as the smell, blood sticking in his mouth.

He held his hand over his face as he stepped around, not wanting to look down, Jack Ng on the floor, a bullet hole in his head, stinking of blood. Jack who used to give him cigars for half price, always talking about his wife, who hadn't made love to him since they left Vietnam.

Stepping on magazines to get around the coroner, the video and player under the counter, why Homicide had called him in. It was an old tape deck, you had to have seen one before to know how to work it, the buttons in a little cabinet in the back, unmarked. The screen came on, white static, Harry rewinding until the store appeared, Don Reedy's face in the lens, pointing a nine-millimeter. Harry watched as Don lowered the gun, stepping backward over the man on the floor, around to the door. Jack Ng stood behind the counter, pointing a little .22, one shot. Then Jack turned his gun to a masked man in the aisle, bang bang, the bullets coming back. Don walked backward out of the store, past Tom Dwight sitting on the floor, blood disappearing into his stomach. Tom jumped to his feet, a loaf of bread in his hand. He placed it on the rack and stepped back to the door, the masked man with him, who had to be Tim, walking out. Jack put his gun under the counter and looked out the window, he turned to the TV next to the register.

Harry played the video forward, back again. Either way it didn't make sense. Jack with his gun out before they even walked in. And why was Tim wearing a mask, Tom not? Fifty thousand dollars in the car, they didn't need this. Harry turned to the TV behind him, which Jack was watching before the twins came in, now off forever with a bullet hole in the center.

The radio started in his car, Harry could hear it beeping from the store, the production company alert system, Miss Delouise calling his number. Carefully he stepped around the coroner, around the counter to the street, the little Delphi they'd lent him, last car on the lot. He got in, Delouise's voice banging on the speakers, saying the tracer on Don Reedy's cell phone had been activated, ten minutes before, one of the robbers, a man named Tom, just used the phone to call his mom. 1313 Lemmings Avenue, Gloria's bar. Harry would be assisting Little Eddy in making the arrest.

"Ten-4," he said, and dropped his head on the seat, too heavy to lift, the rain on the roof, Jack's eyes on the floor, all the mistakes Harry had made in the last two days. If he'd shot

Tim when he had the chance, or arrested Don the day before, cuffed him in the bank the way a cop was supposed to, Jack Ng would still be alive, watching TV, complaining about his wife. If Harry hadn't become a cop here in the first place, hadn't listened to his cousin Henry, a captain over in Vice, always talking about the financial opportunities in Dodgeport policework. Three more years and Harry could retire, spend more time on his writing. That's how he met Loretta, the creative nonfiction class they attended together, the old Widows' Hall on Gambit. She wanted better adjectives for her real estate properties. Harry was going to start a novel.

94

Tim dealt five cards down for Dyan, five for Tom, and five for himself. He yelled out to Rita, her head on her arms at the end of the bar, "You sure you don't want in?" and when she didn't move he picked up his cards and looked at them, and then he picked up Dyan's. "You need two," he said.

Dyan scratched her nose with her shoulder as she watched him deal. She'd been tied to the stool with silver duct tape, silver lines circling her elbows to her ankles, hands taped together taped to her legs taped together. A filthy towel wrapped in tape and tied around her mouth.

"I'll take one," said Tom, who had taped himself to his stool to keep from falling down. The wound in his stomach had stopped bleeding, every now and then oozing a yellowish fluid the color of lager. "I'll bet three hundred," he said, searching his pockets. "Where's my money?"

"I told you already," Tim said. "Don's got the money."

"Where's Don?" Tom asked, his head covered with sweat, running into his eyes. "I thought he was with us."

"No, he's not with us." Tim picked up the cards and threw them down and carried his glass to the bottle next to Rita, pouring it in.

"Where is Don?" Rita said.

"He's coming."

"He's not here?" asked Tom.

"For Christ sake, we're playing cards, aren't we." Tim paced the back of the bar, the bottle to the glass. Then he sat on the cooler, his back to the bar, rocking in the mirror.

Rita stared at the phone in her hand, Don's phone that he'd left there the day before. The last half hour hoping he'd call, hoping Tim was right, that Don would come to the bar. What choice did she have? To go out looking in the street, alone, Crazy Louie's, and if he wasn't there, and if he came to the bar when she was out.

She picked up the phone and threw it at Tim, picking it up again to hit him with it. "You leave him there," punching his arms and ribs, "you left him." Tim's head in his lap, hands wrapped on top, rocking.

"Where could he go? Tell me you would know."

Tim dropped to his knees, the top shelf in front of him, "Try Louie's," he said, a bottle and no glass. "If he's not there, then maybe Iron Heinz."

"Look at that," Tom said, stomach bleeding again, blood on his hands, spreading over the red cards on the bar, kings and queens. "I got a full boat."

Rita ran to the door and opened it, and like clicking a switch, six spotlights went on across the street, the rain making them six thousand, three television cameras underneath, all pointing at Rita. She closed the door and locked it and put her back to it, the phone ringing in her hand. "Hello," she said. "No, Don's not here."

Tim climbed over the bar. "Who is it?"

"The police."

"Let me talk to them. Hello? No, this is Tim. Don is out there and he's got the money and let me just say right now that we're all innocent."

She stepped in front of the window, closing the curtains tighter. "But if they call for Don here that means they do not know where he is."

95

Don lay on Crazy Louie's couch staring up at the colored birds that hung from every corner in the room, little glass birds turning on glass chains, bouncing back the wet lights coming in from the rain. He'd been lying there for an hour, unable to close his eyes, the hole in the old man's head. It was like being back in prison again, rolling in his bed, one cell locked into another. He could leave Louie's apartment anytime he wanted, but for the rest of his life he'd never be able to leave that store, the man lying on the floor.

And there was nothing else he could have done. He knew that now. Because he had tried everything else. He shot the man a dozen times from Louie's couch, shot him everywhere except the head, in the shoulder and the arm, shot the gun right out of his hand. He walked into the store and shot Tim and Tom, shot himself in the head. He dropped his gun and turned around and ran back to the car, to Rita's arms, and then he got up and walked into the store and there was the man on the floor.

Don stood off the couch and found his bag and took out two bundles of hundreds and left them on the table. He pulled one of Louie's sweatshirts over his head and went outside and lit a cigarette, streetlights smelling like dead fish, a big rain coming in. He walked the lines of shadowed pavement, up Thorn to Van Brunt, the hood pulled over his face. So afraid of being caught. He wanted to be caught. He'd do anything to not have to shoot that man again.

Twenty blocks, all the way to Drywell, his old neighborhood, the houses he knew, trying to remember their names, the Nells the Hanleys the Trinkas. Shutters that used to be painted, every one a different color. All the same now, walls peeling gray.

To the fence at the end, pavement driving down into black water, stumps of houses and electric poles. He looked for some sign of the old pier, the bottom of the street, where he and his friends spent entire summers, fishing for crappies, watching for dead bodies. By the time his father was run over, in '71, the pier was already under. That's when the army came in, the dam along Felony that held until Ethel, the hurricane of '75. By the time his mother went with the cancer, the river had risen past the McKennas', his house seized by the state in '83, demolished while Don was serving two years for GLA.

He put his face to the metal wire, the water still several feet from the wall, tide charging in bursts across the macadam, like his parents were still fighting down there. He walked through the zone of empty lots and broken windows, faded ads for cigarettes and bargain cognac. The old longshoremen's hall had been turned into a welfare center, now shuttered, its parking lot half filled with crashed cars. On the sidewalk by the gate, signs for flats fixed, the street down the middle riddled with potholes the size of radials. They built a wall to save a wasteland.

The hookers were still there, three blocks up, staying dry by the pillars under the expressway, twenty or so spread out among the shadowed pilings. No cars. They watched him walk in, asking to see what's in his bag. He didn't know any of them. Ten years a long time here.

"Hey Uncle Don, what you doing?" She stepped into the light, her coat open enough to show a green bra with holes in it. "Don't you remember me? It's Bobbi."

"Jesus Bobbi what are you doing here?"

"You used to come over and swing me around when I was a kid."

"You're still a kid. Where's your father? Where's Big Mike."

"I pretended you were my boyfriend."

"Let's go," he grabbed her coat. "I'm taking you home."

"It's a hundred dollars."

"That's not what I mean. Here," he took a bundle of bills from his bag and shoved it into her hand. "There's five thousand. Okay. You don't have to do this. You get on a plane and you get out of here and you never come back."

Bobbi looked at the money, "Five thousand dollars," she shouted, spreading the bills in front of her, the other women surrounding them, grabbing at his legs, his bag, saying, "Let me take care of you."

He dragged Bobbi's coat toward the alley beneath the factory, the women keeping in a pack behind. A car entered the street from Marginal, its police spotlight sweeping along the pillars, a black Fort Worth coming toward them, the light catching up. At the first burst of siren, he was already running, into the alley and around the trucks in the back, over the loading docks to Lemon.

The unmarked Fort Worth drove between the pillars into the middle of the women and stopped, King's head opening the window. "What the hell is this? You're bunching up again. Come on, spread it out, one to every column." He turned to Arnold in the passenger seat and said, "I swear sometimes they're like sheep."

One of the women ran up to the window, "Some guy just gave Bobbi five grand."

King shined the spotlight ahead, a man running into the factory, Bobbi alone with the glare. He pulled the car forward. "Hey Bobbi, that guy just give you five thousand?"

Bobbi came up to the car, shaking her head. "Who?"

"Come on Bobbi," he held out his hand.

"It wasn't five thousand," she pulled half the bills from her skirt.

"I'm getting wet," King said. She gave him half the rest. "You get his name."

"I don't know. Don something."

"That's what I thought." King turned around to the backseat, Rob Landetta sitting with a camera on his shoulder. "This won't take long, Rob."

96

Tim paced back and forth the length of the bar, stopping in front of Dyan at every pass to shrug or nod or tap her on the arm. His brother Tom had moved to the floor, his back to the wall, a bloody sheet taped in silver around his bulging stomach. Rita wiped at his head with a towel, mopping the cheeks, his bald crown as white as a sink. The phone rang, Don's phone in her hand, 'Hello," she said. "No, who is this. I call three times already where is the help? . . . He's right here," she pushed the phone into Tom's hand, closing his fingers around, raising it to his ear. "Tell them you need the ambulance."

"I got it," Tom said, fighting to lift his head. "Hello? Brian Halo? I'm okay, how are you?" He turned to Rita, "He says it's raining," then back to the phone, wedging it into his collar, hands free to hold in his stomach. "Dyan's right here, she's been great . . . Yes . . . What do I want? Jeez, I got to think." He slid to his back on the floor, calling to his half brother behind the bar. "It's Brian Halo, he says we're on TV."

Tim rummaged behind the bottles for the remote, pointing it at the television above, the picture backing onto the screen, of the bar from across the street, lights on, curtains closed. He raised the volume, Tom's voice on the phone on TV, his list of demands—to see Ted Williams play again, to marry the weather lady on channel 15. A list that seemed to grow faster than Tom could speak: tearful calls for his mother to understand him, for Maureen Trinka, the cashier at Mrs. Donut, to just once in her life say yes, she'd like to have dinner with him. Words running into one another, Tom's sobs at the end, like a fan belt about to snap.

Tim hadn't heard his brother cry since they were kids, thirty years keeping it in, just waiting for someone to ask. The rain on the screen above, tears on Tim's face as he picked up the phone behind the bar, the same one he'd used so many nights before, same number.

"Hello Loretta, it's me Tim, please don't hang up I have to tell you something . . . Listen to me Loretta it's just that I love you baby and I miss you so much . . . I'm not drunk, I'm drinking but I can't get drunk, that's almost the same as not drinking ain't it . . . Don't hang up baby there's something else. I'm on TV. Channel 63. Turn it on . . . You see the bar, that's right, I'm inside. Dyan Swaine is here too, the actress, she's sitting right next to me." Tim patted Dyan's shoulder, her face up to his, eyes so full of hate Tim might as well have been looking at Loretta. "I'm in a lot of trouble here baby it's been a really bad day for me and I don't know if I'm gonna make it for dinner."

Tim walked to the front window, leaning on the curtains, his voice bending. It broke. "I'm not signing those papers Loretta because I still love you, because what we had before. That never goes away, it just gets buried, all this shit. You still love me too, you used to say it every day, remember, you adored me. Tell me how you used to say it, Loretta. Look at me baby and tell me I was somebody." Tim opened the curtains.

When it was over, no one could be sure who fired the first shot, Detective Hammamann or Little Eddy, or any one of the other ten rental cops. It didn't matter, Harry's was the only gun with real bullets, breaking through the window, the beer in Tim's hand, tearing into the dark wood of the bar, the bottles above, the parachutes on the walls, Tim falling to the floor. Silence again. "We got him," Eddy said, running to the door.

"We got nothing," said Harry.

97

Brian Halo plowed into the bar followed by the detective and ten members of camera and crew. He knelt next to Tim, shaking until the eyes opened. "Are you hit?"

Tim nodded, the broken bottle in his hand.

"Your beer was hit?" He turned to Tom, lying on his side, his head in Rita's lap, "What about you?"

"I'm okay," Tom said, raising his hand and watching it fall. "I left out one thing."

"He needs an ambulance," Rita said.

"Who are you?"

"Go to hell."

Halo backed into the middle of the room. "Okay everybody I want a remote control camera over the TV here and one over there and let's get some stronger bulbs behind the bar and a sound check please we're on in ten minutes."

He turned to Dyan, still tied on the stool. "My sun, my beautiful star, you've been so good," loosening the gag at her mouth.

"Thank God," she said.

The bathroom door opened and Eddy popped out. "Right here," Halo said, and pulled a stool next to Dyan, Eddy climbing on, his back pressed against hers, two men from the crew quickly taping round his chest, around hers, taping them together. "Oh Brian no," Dyan moaned. "Oh no I can't I'm so tired please I can't see."

He placed the towel between her lips, tying it back, "That's okay Dyan I'm seeing for you, just one or two more scenes, we're picking up one hundred thousand every quarter." He turned to Eddy, pulling the gun from his taped hand, "And as for you, look what happened you went running in here without thinking and now you're tied up and worst of all the kidnapper's got your gun." Halo held up the nine-millimeter, "Worst thing that can happen to a cop."

"I'll kill him," Eddy said, fighting with the tape at his chest, the men fighting to gag him.

Halo carried the gun to Tim, now standing at the bar, chest bent over it, arms pulled behind his back, Detective Hammamann searching his pockets. "What's this, Lieutenant?"

"I'm arresting him," Harry said, trying to remember where he left his handcuffs. Did he have them in the Delphi, or were they still in the Royale. Too tired to think, like he hadn't slept in a week. The noise from the sound techs, the grips and cameramen running in, wires around his legs. One of the cops outside might have cuffs, or he could get a pair off the props truck.

"Your name's Harry, isn't it," Halo said, his arm heavy around Harry's shoulders. "Let's talk a moment," turning him through the door.

Rita sat on the floor, cops at the windows and at the door, cops on the TV over the bar. It was five o'clock in the morning, the most miserable night of her life, which had started as one of the best. And nothing to do but wait for the end, her headache getting louder with the voice on the screen above, Anthony King's face talking behind the wheel of a police car. Arnold Pascovic sitting in a uniform beside him, snapping peanut shells out the passenger window, the tumbling lights of Lemmings Avenue.

98

"We catch criminals," King said, "we put 'em away." He glanced quickly at the rain-slicked windshield, searching the side window before turning again to Rob's camera in the back, pausing intently there, "And sometimes we get shot doing it."

He held the look an extra second, coolly ignoring the honking on his left before returning his good eye to the front, punching the siren at the red overhead. King believed the best TV cops were the ones who could speak into the camera without trailing their eyes or having to swerve the car. It took some getting used to, especially with the eye patch. A rhythm to it, back to front, saving the best lines for the lens. Actually, it was almost impossible with the eye patch, but King was determined to try. He'd never seen a cop wear one on TV.

"Just look at Don's rap sheet," he went on. "Starts off jacking cars as a juvie, then moving up to armed robbery at knifepoint, robbing banks with a gun, now he's shooting an old man over a loaf of bread, and nowhere to go except more killing." King faced the camera, "Unless we put him away or we kill him, ain't that right, Arnie?"

Arnold was in the middle of opening his tenth bag of peanuts. Where did they come from? "Look out the dog," he said.

King braked, jerking his eye frontward, just enough time to see the dog go under, the dog's owner running alongside, still holding the leash, the animal caught in the bumper. For half a block they kept it up, the owner jogging patiently at first, his leash leading to the front of the car, like he was taking it out for a run. King stepped on the gas, the leash snapping. Arnold opened another bag, "You hit the dog," he said.

Brian Halo's voice started barking in Rob's headphones, "Pause and get off the dog." Rob cut the audio and swung the camera to the rear window, a simple pan of the night streets, tracking to a man walking alone at the edge of the lights, a tall man wearing a hooded sweatshirt, dragging a black bag on his hip. It was a great shot, the man's face in shadow, shoulders bent to his chest. Rob stayed with him, zooming in as the distance between them grew, the man walking up to the dog owner, now sitting dejectedly on the sidewalk, hands raised empty in the rain. The two together, as if joined by the camera, smaller and smaller, until they went to commercial.

99

Don stood over the man and his empty leash as the lights of the Fort Worth turned green and disappeared behind Dyre. The man crying, "My baby. My baby."

Don took a wrap of fifty from his bag, placing it on the ground by the man's feet. Then he walked up the block, a left on Haight, the bag heavier with every step, rocks in there. He killed that man in the store, no amount of cash could buy it back, or anything else he'd done, the life of a dog. He wanted to give the money to Rita, but to do that he'd have to see her, and to see her would only hurt her, because sooner or later everything he touched got bitten.

He passed a doorway piled with shopping bags and wet paperbacks, a man shivering noisily underneath. Don stopped and stared at the blackened feet, the head stuffed into an old airline tote.

He shook the guy and said, "Hey you, wake up, it's your lucky day." He dug into his bag for a fresh bundle, "You just won the Crumbtown lottery," punching it into the man's hand.

"What?" the man lifted his head, making several attempts to lift the rest.

"Five thousand dollars." Don pulled off the wrapper for him, "Tax free."

Misha rose in one motion crossing his legs. "What?" Examining all corners of the bundle before taking off the top bill, sniffing and rubbing it between his thumbs, "I do for this?"

"You spend it," Don said. "You win."

Misha slowly looked left, down the street to the next corner, then right, then up, waiting for something to fall. "I win?"

Don nodded and the man leapt forward, "I win," knocking him backward onto a car, embracing his middle, then his shoulders, kissing each cheek twice, "My friend."

Don shoved him off, "That's enough," the man still kissing. Don pushed again, no power in his arms. He was laughing too hard.

"I pay to kill my wife today," the man said.

"Hey it's your money, but I'd start with some shoes." Don turned and walked up Haight, still laughing, the first time since he'd been with Rita. He couldn't go back to her but at least he'd have this. Before they took him away, he'd give it away, everything.

100

Rita watched the screen above the bar. She saw the car hit the dog, the camera spinning to the rear window, the long night down Lemmings Ave, then closer, to a man walking on the sidewalk, wearing a hooded shirt, carrying a black bag. She recognized the walk first, the lean of him, the way his head fell on her shoulder when they danced. "It's Don," she shouted, and then to herself, It's Don. Already on her feet, picking up her bag, running to the street.

The cops stood outside in a circle of umbrellas, smoking, one of them shouted hey you and another who's that, each waiting for the first to give chase, no one wanting to get his hair wet.

She kicked off her shoes at the corner, up Lemmings her stockings tearing under her feet, slapping through puddles ankle deep. She guessed ten blocks but she couldn't be sure; had to keep slowing down to see, the rain in her face. Past the bank, down the hill, a man sitting on the curb, the one she'd seen on the TV. He wore a dog's leash around his neck, a pile of money at his side, more money spread out on the wet street in front.

"Excuse me," she said, "the man he was here before, with a black sweater on his head. Where?"

The man didn't look up. He took a hundred-dollar bill from the pile and placed it on the street, spreading it flat with his hands.

"He give you this money?"

The man nodded. Spreading another bill down, at least thirty of them on the ground, the shape of a dog.

She ran the rest of Lemmings to the end, the tide coming over the fence, spilling into the street. Lights coming on in the houses over the bay, up the hill where the water couldn't reach, where one morning was like another. She turned and walked back the way she'd come, her arms crossed over her head, checking every street. To Haight where she made a right, running again, her apartment two blocks down.

Misha was sitting in her doorway, counting another pile of wet money. "Misha," she cried, almost hugging him when she saw the bills. "Don was here," she said, again in Russian, "tell me where he went."

"Your little bank robber Don Reedy has not come. But I am going now to pay the man who will kill you both so I can go home."

She grabbed his shoulders and shook him until his Red Sox cap fell over his head. "No, no, Don Reedy is the man who gave you this money. Where did he go?"

"Oh Rita, my wife. Now you have two Don Reedys. How many have there been." He stood next to her, still counting. "Now I see, Don Reedy on the bus in Gorky. Don Reedy the man who fixed the TV."

"I have to find him," she said, running up the block. She turned onto Thorn, the street where Crazy Louie lived, two men in wheelchairs parked in front of the building, both in dark glasses, hand-painted signs chained to their necks—Help the Blind. Each man counting through a pile of big bills.

She pressed the buzzer, banging until Louie's dazed voice told her to hold on. "Don," she cried, running past him into the living room, the stack of bills on the table. Around to the kitchen, the back bedroom.

"He was sleeping on the couch." Louie picked up some money from the table, stuffed the bills into his kimono. He looked at her dress, the stockings torn off her feet. "You need some shoes." He ran to his closet. "What are you like a six?"

She couldn't speak, the pain in her chest forcing her to the couch, out of breath, her hands on her heart trying to slow it down, slowly, "Where did he go?"

Louie came out with three boxes of shoes, pulling the first pair, pushing them on her feet. "Everybody's wearing these." Her head falling back, the TV remote on the table to her left. She clicked the power on, channel 63, the picture from inside the bar, of Tim standing under the camera, staring dumbly at the lens.

101

Harry Hammamann sat in his Delphi, a notebook on his lap, writing his resignation. Brian Halo had just offered him a substantial raise for not arresting Tim, and the long conversation he'd just completed with the production supervisor, Miss Delouise, had helped to clarify Harry's role on the set. A recent edict Harry wasn't aware of, signed shortly before the mayor's death, giving the production companies complete jurisdiction over their sets, as well as the right to establish courts, build prisons. Harry didn't have a problem with that. His reason for quitting rested somewhere else, something he was having trouble explaining.

He tore up the paper and started another, a letter to Loretta. If there was anyone he could tell this to it was her. He stared at the page, five minutes, nothing. He could wait here five years and still the space would be empty. That's why he was leaving, the words were gone. Like a light switched off in a room, that second heart where his language was kept, the drawers full of poems, three of them published, his definitions of love. Harry was dying here.

He left his resignation, his badge on the dash, walking east to the precinct where his own car was parked. He'd drive it to his uncle's place, the other side of the state, a quiet cabin without antennae. Write his letters to her from there, a whole book of them, the words he couldn't say. Looking ahead as he crossed the street, two headlights in the rain, an Eltra coming toward him. He walked faster, running when he saw it wouldn't stop, the car bouncing over the curb, forcing him to the hood. The driver door open, Loretta heeling her way to his side. "Oh Harry," she said, "I came as soon as I saw it. On the TV. Oh you killed him."

She kissed him hard, like a slap. "I missed," he said.

"Oh no," she pushed her finger at his chest, whispering, "Harry you're no good with the pistol." She grabbed for his shirt, and missed, "You've got to use the rifle," punching his arms. "Oh Harry for chrissakes get it over with."

102

Tim stared at the picture of himself on the screen, hands in his pockets, leaning on the bar. He turned to the camera above the

TV, took his hands out of his pockets, back and forth, sitting on the stool, standing. He smiled, then frowned, then turned around, his brother Tom on the floor behind him. "Tom, what am I feeling here?"

Tom lay on his side, the blood in a pool to his neck, the soft cervical collar acting like a sponge. "Tom, did you hear what I said? What are you looking at?" Tim stepped over to his brother, bending his head next to Tom's, eyes turned up at the ceiling. "I don't see it." He shook Tom's elbow and neck, then put his arm under his brother's head, pulling him onto his lap. "What's wrong?" He lifted his beer and poured it over Tom's lips, down his shirt. Tim turned to the camera above, "I need help here," he said. "Please get my brother an ambulance." The picture on the screen below, of King driving the Fort Worth.

103

King drove slowly, keeping to the right side of the street. Every person they passed Arnold shook his head and said, "That's not him," until King had to yell at him to stop. He held the wheel straight, turning to the camera behind them. "This is the best job in the world," he said, "and sometimes it's the worst. And that's just the way I like it." He turned back to the road just in time to hit the brakes. A man standing in front of them, waving a handful of money.

"That's not him," said Arnold.

Misha came to the window, speaking in Russian. Arnold waved him off. "Drive away," he said to King. "I know who this person is. He wants to pay me to kill his wife."

Misha pulled out another handful of bills, all hundreds. "Wait a minute," King said. "Let's hear what the man has to say."

104

Rita sat on the couch in Louie's apartment shouting at Misha on the TV, the lies he was telling. "I wasn't in bed with Don Reedy. That wasn't Don Reedy."

Louie came out of the bathroom with a blow dryer and pointed it at her ear. "You're going on TV," he said, "you always look your best." Outside in the street a car alarm started to ring, followed by a loud cheer, as if a vandals' parade was passing through. Rita went to the window; ten people out there now, standing on the steps, the two blind men leaving their wheelchairs to stand with the rest, together raising their arms, shouting "Throw it. Throw it here," falling over each other as the bills fell, the money separating in the wind, hands running to catch it, to the ground, shouting for more.

She ran into the hall, up the stairs two at a time. Of course he was here, the sick lady's apartment. By the third landing she could hear the music, Duke Ellington.

105

Don looked back at the TV, a commercial for the gates of heaven. He grabbed a pack of bills and pulled off the wrapper and threw the money out the window, far as he could. Cars stopping, people running in from both sides of the street, all the losers and freaks, the bad breath and smelly feet, sons and daughters of Crumbtown. He threw another handful, watching them run, another. "More," came the screams from below. "More more more."

"Don," she said, the voice from his grave, in the door, in the room, kissing him as he turned. The touch of her hair, the breath of her ear, forgiving him for leaving, for thinking he could stay away. "I love you," he said, her arms in his back. "I love you," she said, tying his legs, his knees to the floor, the bulge of her skirt, more more more.

She pushed him back, "Look." He looked in her eyes, staring at the TV, breaking from his arms to stand at the screen. "They're coming."

106

Rob got out of the car first, the camera panning the street, the people massed at the steps, their arms up the line of windows to Don on the top floor. Rob waved to King and Arnold to get out, tracking them around to the front of the car, guns over their heads as they moved through the crowd. Rob raised the camera again, zooming in on Don's face, the money coming down, the hysterical crowd, cops swinging their guns to get through, heads and backs and arms to the front door, King shooting the lock, holding it open, "After you, partner."

107

Don walked on his knees to the TV. He turned it off. "There's nothing on." He grabbed her ankle and kissed her shin, "Let's go to bed."

"No, they are coming," she ran to the door, looking down the stairs. "Please, we have to go," running back to him, pulling his hand as hard as she could, whispering, "Now."

Up the stairs to the roof, the island of twisted steampipe, an abandoned chicken coop, a wooden rowboat full of holes. To the edge, no fire escape, the crowd erupting when Don looked down. He reached for another bundle and threw it over the side.

"Don please," she said as Arnold and King came firing through the door. They fell together, rolling over one another to get behind the old boat, Don holding her head as he shot back. Three, then two more, bullets beating on the pipes.

He pulled out the clip. Four left. Firing the one in the chamber. Three. When Arnold and King finished shooting back, he kissed Rita once behind the ear and with the clip still out he squeezed the trigger, click click click.

"What's that?" King raised his head. "Did you hear that, partner?"

"No bullets?" Arnold stood, the two men stepping around the pipes, their guns pointed at the empty boat, Don and Rita behind.

"Man's out of bullets," said King. "Man's out of time."

Rob kept the two men centered in the frame as he moved right, his eye never leaving the lens, the shot of them coming toward the camera. Everything was perfect, the rain soaking into the tarp, the black angled piping, background calls of the crowd. From the moment he stepped from the car, Rob and his machine were one, through the people on the street, the money falling out of the air. This was how he started in the business, a cameraman, nineteen years old, his first love, the eye to the lens, the lens the world; everything passing through, existing by his will.

He shifted the camera, focusing on Arnold now, on the big man's chest, a gunshot cracked from behind, a red circle in the jacket. Arnold dropped his gun to the roof, dropping to his knees. Rob pointed the camera at King, another gunshot, King looking at his own shoulder, taking a seat to study more carefully, one hole, another crack, the hole below. King moved his gun to his left hand and fired up in the air, fired at the roof, then, steadying it one final shot, directly at the camera.

Rob looked at the sky, a darkening ocean, rain falling on the lens, no longer fighting to keep it off, drops bouncing off the glass. It made for a beautiful shot, a better finish than he could have thought, thunderclouds at the bottom of the sea. Rob saw Don's and Rita's legs stepping over him, the sound of their feet on the stairs going down, then the silent arms of the water lifting him up, holding him close above the world, floating into black, widening the unlimited, the big picture.

108

Eddy twisted back and forth against Dyan, his wooden stool banging on the bar's floor, arms twitching like he'd been plugged into the wall. Of all the roles he'd played today, this one came easiest, a part he'd been playing his whole life, the trapped animal, the wolf in the net. No acting to it, no thought, only instinct, writhing violently against the tape.

Dyan elbowed him in the ribs, shouting through the gag in her mouth, "You're hurting me." Eddy froze, panting dryly a few seconds. Then howling as he bent her forward, wriggling up her back, inching himself through the tape at his chest. He bent her further, her head against the bar, the tape sliding down to his stomach, stuck around his hips.

Dyan bucked once, twice, she'd had enough, driving her head into his face, her elbows against his legs. Eddy tilted over, pivoting around the tape at his waist, still wrapped around her chest. His head swung to the bottom of her chair, his hairless legs rising up from his pants, clapping around her head, tightening the tape severely between her ribs. She couldn't breathe. He was killing her.

His face at her feet, the towel loosed from his mouth, he reared backward and began gnawing at the tape around her ankles, that still connected her to the stool. In a moment he was through. Dyan stood, the seat falling between them, Eddy upside down at her back, suspended from the tape at her chest, his legs crossed over her face.

She stumbled forward, then back, toppling stools and tables, into the fabricked wall. She lunged at the bar, then back to the wall, as hard as she could, trying to break him off. Eddy grunting as his head hit the baseboard. "Again," he said.

109

Tim knelt over his brother. "Tom," he pleaded, "talk to me." He placed his hand over Tom's eyes and brushed them closed and looked up at the TV, his own eyes half shut from crying, straining to see the picture of himself crying on the screen, his brother on the floor.

There was a loud thud behind, Eddy hitting the wall one more time.

"Stop that," Tim said. "Have a little respect." He lifted his brother's hands and folded them over the chest, his arms under Tom's neck and waist, lifting him up, stumbling to the TV, shouting at the screen, "It's your fault." Then forward to the shattered window, all the strength he had left, the faceless cameras across the street, and there, to the right and behind, his wife Loretta, standing with the detective, twenty feet away. "Loretta," he cried, "help me baby I don't know what to do," shaking his brother in his arms, "Come on," kissing his cheek, "oh Tom."

110

Loretta took one step forward, a reflex from twelve years of marriage, before stopping herself and turning to the man at the cameras, as if they could change what she'd just seen. It was supposed to be Tim. Harry shot the wrong man. She looked again at Tom's blood-soaked shirt, Loretta backing into the building behind her. All the mistakes she'd made in her life, which started the day she met Tim. She'd taken him back so many times, and she knew if he kept asking she'd take him back again, the one thing she couldn't bear. His heart broken on the phone, lying on the front steps, flowers in his hand, begging her forgiveness. Who was going to forgive Loretta?

111

Brian Halo sat on the floor in the back of Truck One, tears running over his eyes, into his mouth, laughing in great bursts as Eddy's taped hands became caught between Dyan's legs, his head hitting the wall as Tim cried his brother's name. "It's so sad," Halo moaned, "it's so funny," wiping his eyes as he pushed himself to the door, his crew in front of him. "We did it," he said, "we did it," like he'd just invented a new pill.

Detective Hammamann stepped into the middle of the street, facing the window, the rifle in his arm. He raised it to his shoulder, pointing at Tim inside. "My God no," Halo said, running up and tackling the officer from behind, fighting for the gun.

Harry pulled the rifle free, butting Halo in the head. Up to his shoulder again, looking for Tim in the sights and finding Loretta, her arms around her husband, and a sound he'd never heard before, Loretta crying. He lowered the barrel to her chest, the two of them joined in the window, tears in Harry's eyes as he felt for the trigger, hands shaking, he didn't want this, squeezing as someone tackled him from the side, the rifle shooting out of his hands, into the air. Harry lay on his back, looking up at Don over his chest. "Thank you," Harry said, "I quit."

Don picked up the rifle and turned to Rita, two steps to her arms, "Where's the car?"

"In the alley," she said, "behind the bar."

A cheer struck from down the street as the crowd turned the corner and spied Don holding the bag. Their numbers had grown to more than two hundred, many of them sick and injured, crippled and bedridden. Even Big Debbie had joined in, so fat she hadn't left her bed in three years, and had recently been featured in a commercial for construction equipment.

Into the set, toppling cameras, overturning a coffee truck. Brian Halo running toward them, his arms wide, crying "Wait, wait," his suit disappearing at their feet. Don opened the bag, the last two bundles. He threw up one, then the other, then he threw the bag. Windows smashed, light poles exploding where they fell, crowd and crew fighting for the bills, tearing at the ground like starving gulls. When the street was picked clean they flooded into the bar, sweeping Eddy and Dyan before them, Tim and Tom and Loretta, pushing them to the rail, their money raised high, shouting "Bartender, bartender."

Don and Rita ran to the alley, splashing through water over their feet. The Bollinger whined when he touched the wires, then kicked in suddenly, dragging them backward into Van Brunt, the green lights on Lemmings to the water risen half a block over the sandbagged fence. A right on Drywell, up Marginal to the pylons of the expressway, the long ramp circling to the top, clouds breaking over. When the city was behind them he reached for her knee, driving the warmth of her leg. She kissed his shoulders with her cheek and in less than a minute she was asleep.

He got off the highway in Seagram, onto 25 that used to be a flea market and was now eight lanes, cement blocks of every width. He couldn't think about anything except keeping his eyes open, his hands awake, the sleep after the dream is done. They drove through the Morgans, town and ville and field. It stopped raining and the sun cracked in and the trees moved up to the side of the road to block it out. Rita lifted her head and pulled in her hair. "I'm hungry," she said.

He ordered the Tomahawk Scramble and she had the Indian Toast. He poured ketchup over everything. "I dreamed," she said. "It was a good dream. I was telling you of another dream, like I am telling you now but we were in bed in a bedroom that's where we lived and in the dream the dream I was telling it was about these things that happen to us, how we meet and robbing the bank and the television show and escape and then I am finished and you laugh and you say that is a good dream Rita and you put your hand right there."

"Right there."

"Yes, right there."

"And then what."

"I don't remember."

"Try to remember," he wiped some dark toast from her lip.

She looked at the tables next to them, everyone sleeping, snoring while they ate. "I love your hand."

"Let's find that room."

"Maybe it was in the house where we're going, the Gale."

"Someplace closer."

"The Las Vegas," she said.

He picked up the check, watching her the whole time, trying not to blink. Every breath she took he took two. "In this dream were we rich?"

"No."

"It's true," he said, holding up two singles.

"No, it is okay," reaching into her bag, a stack of credit cards.

The Las Vegas was ten miles up the Post. A neon tail fin leaning over the road: gold coins falling on a green blonde, day rates and clean beds. The man watching the TV in the office wore a pink turban over a Hawaiian shirt. He glanced at Don and Rita coming through the door, then back to the TV, a picture of Dyan Swaine driving a police car, Little Eddy riding next to her. "Don't hurt me," the man said, and pulled a shotgun from under his desk. Don smacked the barrel down as he rolled over the counter, taking the man to the floor. He came up with the gun, pulling Rita out the door, the man following with a pistol, shooting at the car.

112

Little Eddy and Dyan Swaine drove into the Las Vegas an hour later, responding to a call from the motel. They waited for the camera trucks to unload, then they got out of the car and walked toward the owner, who was sweeping up the remains of his door.

Little Eddy drew his gun and crouched down, "Freeze," he said. "Drop the broom."

"What are you doing, Eddy?" Dyan walked over to him. "You're so stupid."

"I get the reward?" the owner said.

"Just step away from the broom," Eddy said. "That's real good." He spit on the ground, wiped his mouth with his gun.

"Pig," Dyan said.

Eddy lowered his gun, "I'm sorry."

She held his head with her arms, "It's okay. You're gonna be okay."

113

In the back of Truck One Brian Halo pointed at Screen Three as he yelled into Phone Five. "Look at them together. Look at them, Dyan and Eddy. Did I tell you these two have chemistry? You can't take us off. We got a seven-point rating for that scene in the bar and it's still picking up. The girl has the phone. We can trace it if they answer. We're right behind them. Enough?" He threw the phone in the box in the corner and picked up another from the basket by his chair. "Get me Don Reedy."

114

They drove through the dead trees of Keene County, miles without seeing a house. Rita stared out the window, her head pressed into the seat. They hadn't spoken since the Las Vegas, and she didn't know how to begin.

Her bag began to ring. "It's your phone," she lifted it out. "Hello?" covering it with her hand. "Don, are you here?"

"What?" he said, like he'd been talking to the engine.

"The phone," she held it over his nose. "It's for you."

. . .

When it was over, Don threw the phone out the window, smashing it against a telephone pole. "That was Brian Halo. He wants us to rob a show in North-Central, it's all set up, some general store in a talking-cow show. They're gonna leave five thousand in the register." He turned to Rita, "We can keep robbing stores on TV. He says it will be okay. I shot that man, Rita."

"It wasn't your fault."

And he explained to her how it was, the prison sentences that kept getting longer, "It wasn't your fault," she said.

Don remembered the driveway behind the turn, the first hundred yards barely drivable, then two miles of paved road to the top of the hill. He'd only been to the Gail once, twelve years before. Maury had brought him there to talk about the bank robberies, and as a way of showing Don that he was second-in-command, next in line. Maury said he'd only shown the Gail to four other people, all of them murdered shortly after.

"The Gale?" asked Rita. "Like a storm?'

Don nodded, "The Gail was Maury's mom."

They rounded the last curve to the top, the house built like a bunker, concrete walls with foot-high windows, a single door of steel rivets. Don went to the elm that hung over the barbed wire roof. He climbed a branch, reaching up and back. "The key's still here."

"He built this for his mother?" she asked.

Don nodded. "To keep her out."

. . .

He started the generators, the lights flickered and held, electric torches on wrought iron chandeliers, the main hall decorated like a dungeon. He led her down the stairs, the ice room and pantry, enough wine and food to keep them drunk and fed for years. There was no way to trace the place to Maury. It was owned by a Mr. Minanski, who Maury claimed was buried throughout the house.

Don brought two beers back and sat on the plastic-covered couch and watched her walk around the hall, her torn stockings, telling him about growing up in Odessa, sharing three rooms with ten people, one bathroom for twenty. It was all about curtains, she said, already she knew how to fix it. She'd plant a garden, fresh vegetables in the summer, her grandmother had a farm outside Odessa and the whole family would take the bus there every weekend. She opened a beer and carried it to the hall in the corner. She winked at Don and said, "What is this," and went in.

She was sitting on the bed when he came in, blankets of battleship gray. Over the headboard a giant portrait, of an angry Gail in a red and gold robe.

He moved along the wall, the concrete against his back, until he stood across from where she sat, his hand climbing to the short window behind his head, feeling for the bulletproof glass. She leaned toward him, her arms under her shoulders like she was about to start rowing. This was his moment, to fall into her again, the way they'd fallen before, as easy as getting into bed. He stepped forward, then hesitated, a fraction of a second but she saw it and he saw her see, and she rowed back to bed alone, her elbows holding her up.

"I'll check the alarms," he said, "be right back." The door

was stuck and he finally opened it and went into the hall and drank some whiskey and when he returned she was asleep. He sat next to her, tracing her body with his finger in the sheets, remembering her dream, the same one that he killed the old man in, one and the same. All of it outside now, the concrete walls of the Gail, windows you couldn't open, sheets on the bed as heavy as cement. They'd be starting with nothing, only the weight of what happened, build their own world, block by block. He'd led her here, now she would lead. She'd sew the curtains, collect the eggs from the cows. The garden would grow. He lay his head by hers and touched her lips, watching her sleep.

115

Joe Far came to work that morning to find two hundred men and women stuffed into the long space of the bar waiting with large bills for someone to get them a drink. He ran out to the street half a block before the crowd caught up and carried him back, passing him over their heads, one to the other, over the bar where he began to pour.

It was a wake for Tom and a going-away-to-jail party for Tim, a salute to their hero, Don Reedy, and to themselves and their fortune, to live in the greatest city in the world. The party lasted seven days, the second longest in memory, rivaled only by the sinking of the casino Clementine, in '84. By the third day the floodwaters had reached the door, bringing more people in, a steady stream of ambulances taking them out, more than thirty people hospitalized, all in serious condition, all returned. Even Tom, who despite every incompetence by the staff at Mercy was revived and twenty-four hours later drove himself backward to his own wake.

Tim would remember those days as the happiest in their marriage. Loretta never looked more beautiful, with the lights from the water on the floor, Crazy Louie's fox draped over her arm. Loretta's sweater. Loretta smiling. Everyone smoking. Tim raised his glass and said, "Who's better than us?" He climbed up to the bar, threw the glass against the wall. "Who's better than us?" he shouted. The crowd answering as one.

116

Don woke first, evening light. He slipped out of bed and quietly put on his pants and shoes, his jacket from under the chair. He wouldn't be able to do this while she was awake, didn't have the words. He went back to the bed and kissed her once more and walked to the door. The door was stuck.

She opened her eyes. "You are going?"

He yanked it open, searching the hall. "I was going to walk."

"You are walking how far."

"I don't know." He went to the bed, on his knees holding her hand. "The longer you're with me the more trouble you're in. They'll find us here, Rita, they always do." He stood, trying to let go. "You can still get away."

"I am coming with you."

"There's no place to go."

Her hands pressed into the bed, "Okay." She stood and walked to the other room, to the phone on a stand next to the couch. He watched her from the hall, dialing, waiting, "New

York City," she said, "*Brian Halo Show* producer." Dialing some more, "Hello, I have Don Reedy here and I must speak with Brian Halo," waiting, "Yes, I am with Don Reedy" . . . "Hello, this is Brian Halo" . . . "Yes, so when that we rob this store . . ."

He came up behind her, grabbing her by the waist, the two of them falling in the couch. "Yes," she said, "okay, yes, tomorrow afternoon . . ." Kissing her ear in the phone, the lake of her neck, endless again.

A Note About the Author

Joe Connelly is the author of *Bringing Out the Dead,* which was made into a film by Martin Scorsese. A native of New York City, he now lives in the Adirondacks with his wife and family. *Crumbtown* is his second novel.

A Note on the Type

This book was set in Bodoni, a typeface named after Giambattista Bodoni (1740–1813), the celebrated printer and type designer of Parma. The Bodoni types of today were designed not as faithful reproductions of any one of the Bodoni fonts but rather as a composite, modern version of the Bodoni manner. Bodoni's innovations in type style included a greater degree of contrast in the thick and thin elements of the letters and a sharper and more angular finish of details.

Composed by Stratford Publishing Services,
Brattleboro, Vermont
Printed and bound by R. R. Donnelly,
Harrisonburg, Virginia
Designed by Virginia Tan